Beauty in Pain

Also by Alice Benton

Poetry

Black Love: A Book of Poetry & Love

Beauty in Pain

Alice V. Benton

iUniverse, Inc.
Bloomington

Beauty in Pain

iUniverse books may be ordered through booksellers or by contacting:

iUniverse
1663 Liberty Drive
Bloomington, IN 47403
www.iuniverse.com
1-800-Authors (1-800-288-4677)

ISBN: 978-1-4620-2888-7 (pbk)
ISBN: 978-1-4620-2890-0 (cloth)
ISBN: 978-1-4620-2889-4 (ebk)

Printed in the United States of America

iUniverse rev. date: 06/15/2011

All Glory to God!

TO ALL THOSE
WHO WENT ABOVE & BEYOND
WHAT WAS NECESSARY

JMP

Foreword

ALICE Benton was my student advisee when she attended college in Brooklyn, NY. She was also the most efficient work study assistant that the department of social science has ever had. Therefore, I should not have been surprised at her competence after reading her second work and initial foray into narrative prose, **Beauty in Pain.** In her follow up to **Black Love: A Book of Poetry & Love**, Ms. Benton confronts a topic that all people will eventually have to encounter: the mortality of someone held dear. Because she is not a trained psychologist or social worker, Alice weaves the inter-relationships and inter-connectedness of one family confronting life's eventuality without therapeutic assertions.

Familial antagonisms, unknowingly hurtful words spoken by friends, and the need to love self prior to loving others, are common issues that many families confront when dealing with the issue of a dearly departed loved one. Ms. Benton addresses these topics so well in her narrative that the reader will be disappointed after reading the last chapter. The disappointment will be that the reader will want to read more! This is the mark of a good writer.

Alice Benton is a very spiritual person; she is a loving mother, a good friend and a honest and decent person. I know this as a result of interacting with her for almost a decade. What I have found out about her recently, by re-reading her current work, is that she writes her ass off. Like me, you will read **Beauty in Pain** and anxiously await her next publication, **Autumn's Five Seasons.** Write on, my Sister!

Professor James R. Allen, Chairperson
Social Science Department
School of New Resources
College of New Rochelle

Acknowledgments

IN the name of the Father, the Son and the Holy Spirit; all things are possible through Christ. This book has truly been a labor of love. Love of family. Love of friends. Love of caring strangers. Love of former co-workers. Love of life and lessons learned. I offer special blessings to my entire family, the SunTrust Family, Concierge Innovations, Bed, Bath & Beyond, EZ, Dr. James Allen and Ms. Marilyn Beckford.

I also acknowledge the beauty I have found in my pain and the wisdom to know I should do something with it. We do not get to choose how we obtain our blessings, but it is our personal responsibility to take heed and recognize them.

This book was inspired by a true event that has given me some knowledge through experience, but I am in no way offering professional solace. Please obtain suitable help when necessary.

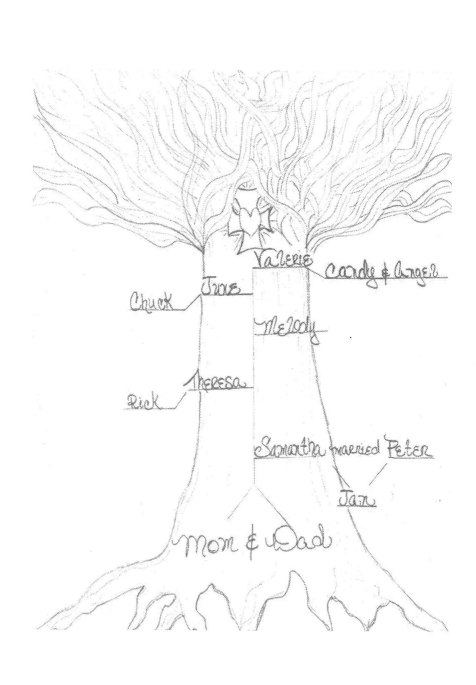

Prologue

IT was an early Saturday morning and June had just kissed her son, Chuck. She headed out the door because of work and walked to the car.

June said, "Thanks for making breakfast."

June was on to him, Chuck wanted to borrow the car for a party later in the evening. She noticed all the hints he had been giving her about it all week.

"I love you, ma, you're the best!" Chuck yelled.

"I know and I love you too."

June smiled and sat in her car adjusting the mirrors. *Why can't Chuck leave my mirrors alone? I know he's over six feet, but come on.* She glanced at him in the rearview mirror. He was standing near the front door waving.

I can't believe he's eighteen. I remember his birth like it was yesterday. June recalled being pregnant and rushing into the car with three out of four of her sisters, Samantha, Melody and Theresa. Samantha kept saying, "Do what I say and everything will be alright."

The sound of June's cellular phone ringing interrupted her nostalgic thought.

Chuck asked, "Is everything alright? You're gonna be late ma."

She answered, "I'm fine, but you're right, I have to go. I'll call you later." *June thought, I'm tired, but thankful to finally be on the road. I just want to get this day over with so I can go back home and rest.*"

As soon as June said those words, a car came from nowhere and crashed into her vehicle.

Part One

The Accident

Chapter 1

VALERIE was in the middle of a good dream when she heard her ten year old daughter, Candy speaking. Candy's voice was very faint and sweet, but soft which is why she could hardly hear it. Valerie had fallen into an unusually deep sleep on the living room couch.

Candy said, "Mommy, mommy."

Valerie lifted her head instinctively, but barely opened her eyes wanting desperately to go back to sleep. Her head dropped.

"Mommy," Candy said again pausing and then she screamed, "Valerie!"

Valerie lifted her head and said, "I know I didn't just hear you call my name. What'd you call me?" She said sternly and without thought before dropping her head and closing her eyes again.

"June's been in a car accident," Candy said.

Suddenly, the words registered and Valerie sat up and questioned, "What? My sister what?" but Candy was gone. Valerie screamed, "Candy! Candy! What did you say about June?"

Candy came back into the living room and said, "Chuck called and said his mother was in a bad accident. He's talking to mom. They're on the phone, but I think you need to get up."

There was something about the way Candy said, "I think you need to get up." Those words hit her like a ton of bricks. Valerie immediately sprung up off the sofa to go ask mom what happened, but mom was already coming down the stairs with Samantha.

It's strange how things work out sometimes. Samantha never spent the night in Brooklyn. Whenever she came over she would always be in a hurry to rush home to her husband. Last night was different for some reason. Samantha came over and announced she was here for the weekend.

Valerie sarcastically joked, "Are you serious? Your husband is letting you stay out? I didn't know Peter could survive being in New Jersey alone."

"Ha, ha, ha. Very funny." Samantha replied, mockingly.

In fact, talking to Samantha was why Valerie was so out of it and couldn't crawl up the stairs to her bedroom last night. Samantha's stay was so bizarre they stayed up all night talking and drinking red wine.

Samantha and mom came into the living room. Mom said "Valerie, June's been in a car accident and Chuck says it was bad. He's trying to get to the hospital. Theresa was left a message and Melody will be there tomorrow."

"Thank God Theresa lives in Georgia too. So Chuck won't be alone. How did Chuck find out?"

Samantha answered, "A chaplain went to the house to notify her family."

"A chaplain?" Valerie questioned.

"Yes, a chaplain." Samantha repeated.

Valerie began to involuntarily picture loved ones passed on, one after another. They were everywhere simply standing in and about the room looking onward. Although Valerie found these images warming, they were also disturbing. First, she saw her grandparents, then various aunts and uncles. She did her best to ignore them, trying to stay focused on the issue at hand asking, "What hospital is she in?"

Mom let out a sad exaggerated gasp before answering. She said, "June was taken to Douglasville County Hospital but should have been taken to Grady because of the trauma she experienced."

The chaplain is taking Chuck to the hospital. He took him to the hospital and they arranged to have June moved to Grady Hospital by helicopter.

Valerie called Grady Hospital to obtain an update about June, but got nothing. Someone answered quickly, but when they transferred her to the trauma emergency line she was placed on hold. While listening to Grady's telephone recording about the hospital, which seemed to last a lifetime, she learned a little information. It mentioned how the hospital services most of Atlanta's ambulance needs and how they were best in dealing with traumatic injuries. *Valerie thought, I guess June's in the right place.*

"Hello, how may I help you?" the hospital clerk said.

"Hi, my name is Valerie Peterson. My sister, June Peterson, was brought to your emergency room and I would like an update on how she's doing."

"Please hold." The clerk said. She returned less than a minute later saying, "I'm sorry Ms. Peterson, I can't say much on the phone, but a June Peterson was brought into the trauma emergency room and is being operated on as we speak. Also, it's absolutely imperative that a family member be available inside of the hospital for decisions."

Chuck and the chaplain couldn't move as fast as the helicopter, but they were on the way.

Valerie asked, "What kind of decisions need to be made?"

"Sorry, ma'am, that too cannot be discussed over the telephone. We need someone here in the hospital."

"Alright, her adult son is on his way."

Theresa first found out June was in a car accident through voicemail. Samantha called her, but could not get through, so she left a message. Theresa heard the house phone, but she had things on her mind and ignored it. Then her cell phone rang. She let it go to voicemail. *They'll leave a message if it's important.* When the message tone blurted she freaked and instantly called to listen to the message.

It was then that Theresa heard Samantha's voice telling her about their little sister, June. Theresa tried to reach Chuck, but couldn't until later. When they finally spoke, Chuck was already at the hospital.

Theresa asked, "When are visiting hours?"

Chuck screamed, "Just come now! I don't know how much time you have!"

Theresa dropped everything and began running frantically to the nearest bus stop. She reached it in no time. The bus doors were closing when she lodged her hands between them attempting to pry them open. Theresa wasn't strong enough, but wasn't going to let go even if it forcibly dragged her away from the curb. "I can't miss this bus!" she screamed angrily.

The driver let her board the bus, but that's when Theresa realized she had no change. She dashed quickly forgetting to get coins. The severity of the situation began to hit and she cried hysterically at the thought of having to get off the bus. She pleaded, "I need to get to Grady Hospital. Please don't kick me off the bus. I have to get there now."

The driver said, "Don't worry. I'll get you there."

The ride was long, but she finally reached Five Points. The bus let Theresa off right in front of the hospital. Once inside, Theresa walked all over the emergency room peeking in on people trying to locate June. Eventually, she found June in a recovery room. Theresa took one look at her sister and cried."

Back in Brooklyn, it was time to head for Georgia. The family rapidly made plans to be at June's side. The earliest available flight was at 1:00 p.m. That would leave just enough time to pack and go.

The doorbell rang and Valerie ran to open the door. It was Peter and he was crying. He said, "Chuck told me that June hasn't had any brain activity for at least forty minutes. This is really serious."

Peter and Samantha had been together for a long time. They were that neighborhood couple that seemed like they had always been dating. In grade school, Peter took one look at Sam and said, "You're mine." And that was it. She was his. They've been together ever since. So he's been a part of the family longer than all the other siblings. He truly is like a brother.

Yet, in all that time, Valerie had never seen Peter cry, at least, not until today. This was the first time, Saturday, April 22, 2006, leaning against the door in the foyer. Peter was delivering the worst news ever and sobbing. Valerie was shocked at first, but shouldn't have been because he and Sam helped to take care of June.

Peter went upstairs and repeated what he just said to his father-in-law, "dad", as everyone called him. Peter left it to dad to tell "mom," as everyone called his mother-in-law. Peter went and told his wife and daughter, Jan. Samantha swiftly said she couldn't go to Georgia, but would send Peter to represent her branch of the family tree.

Samantha and Jan would stay home with all the children and dad. *Samantha thought Jan and I can lean on each other.* The pair would comfort and take care of the homebound family. They would hold it together for the children.

Peter parked his car in the garage and they caught a cab to the airport. Mom and Valerie carried rosaries in hand. Mom also had prayer cards and a Bible. Valerie was sitting between mom and Peter feeling pressure from each side. That's when she realized that she was physically holding them up. *Valerie wondered, who's gonna keep me from falling.* They were already well on the way.

Usually, the trip to Georgia wasn't a bad one, but this time they needed to get there extra fast. Earlier, they were awakened about 7:30 a.m. and half the day had passed. The flight was delayed repeatedly. They didn't make it to Atlanta's Hartsfield Airport until about 6:00 pm. Going up those long escalators in the airport on the way to baggage claim, Valerie began to experience a horrid feeling. Never before had she been in this airport without June being around.

June was usually near the escalators, always waiting somewhere nearby. The last time Valerie visited with mom and her children, June was there waiting. She wasn't in the usual spot, though—at the top of the escalators, she was kind of far away. Valerie looked around and wondered what happened, as she turned right to go toward the baggage claim. As Valerie approached, she noticed this beautiful girl smiling. The girl leaped forward and gave her a hug. It was June! Generally speaking, June was a looker, but today she looked radiant. She was beaming from head to toe.

Now, on the day of the accident, it was different. June wasn't in the airport and she wasn't coming. Subconsciously, Valerie began to visually search for June. Instead, she saw her nephews, Chuck and Rick. They never picked her up, so as they emerged, her heart slowly continued to break.

Chuck and Rick looked different. They hugged and kissed their aunt, but it wasn't the same as it had been in the past. Typically, Chuck's big beautiful eyes would be bright and he'd just walk up with wide arms and immediately give a huge embrace and kisses to everyone. Whereas, Rick would display a faint version of his gorgeous smile and wait to be embraced because "the kid", as he would often call himself, prefers the attention to be brought to him. Their faces had a strange uncomfortable look in different ways. They both immediately gave a light hug and said they were glad the family made it safely.

There they were again. Valerie could see our family members who passed on standing in the airport. They were watching and moving in perfect step with everyone. Valerie's sightings were increasing. She couldn't get them out of her mind. She desperately wanted them to go away, but they hadn't. It bothered Valerie because it felt as if they were all going to see June, both the living and the dead. Some would be saying goodbye and others would be welcoming her home.

Valerie decided to go and help mom and Rick get the bags at baggage claim. As Valerie approached, she started to wonder what she packed. Let's face it, this was no vacation and she really wasn't paying attention. The goal was to skip town as soon as possible and that mission was accomplished. *The clothes were definitely mix matched and no shoes were packed.* A black sneaker-shoe styled Diesel adorned her feet and that was fine. They weren't here for a fashion show and the quick exit was necessary.

Rick walked up to Valerie slowly. He spoke to his aunt as if in denial. Rick said "Aunt June is really bad. She's swollen and everything is too big. Her eyes and tongue look like they're coming out of her head and every now and then she blinks unnaturally. Oh, and her eye has a hole off to the side of it."

Valerie looked at Rick in desperation and said, "Please tell me that's not what you were just saying to my mother."

He said, "No, but I don't know if mom will be able to handle it. June's hooked up to a lot of machines."

Peter saw Rick in his urban gear and went crazy. He started yelling, "Pull up your pants boy! Pull up your pants!"

Chuck said, "You know how his style is Peter." Chuck tried to lighten the mood further saying, "Maybe we can stop at a store and buy him some suspenders."

Joking didn't work because Peter was full of rage. He attempted to charge Rick in the airport, in the parking lot and once again while they were riding in the van. Peter even yelled at Chuck in the worst ways while he drove . . . Chuck . . . whose mother was fighting for her life. Peter was riding shotgun and Rick was in the back of the van. The distance from the airport to the hospital wasn't far, but that was a long explosive ride.

When they finally made it to the hospital Chuck helped mom out of the van on the left side. Peter got out on the right and stood there with an indescribable look on his face. Valerie was seated behind Peter and also got out on the right side of the van. Rick exited from the back on the right and Peter charged again. Valerie yelled, "No one is going to hit them today, especially not Chuck, not during this tragedy." She leaned back in toward the van and slammed the sliding door shut. That's when Peter started screaming at Valerie and hit her hard making her fall in the street.

While he was screaming, Valerie flashed back to a younger time. She remembered spilling some juice on the kitchen floor and Peter yelling at her for being sloppy. He literally grabbed Valerie by the hair and forced her to sit down on the floor. Peter dragged her across the kitchen floor; wiping the mess up with her body. Valerie cried as she tried to loosen his grip while trying to keep the hair close to her head to lessen the pain. She went back and forth over the tile becoming soiled by the juice. Afterward, Peter laughed, "Next time you'll be more careful. Won't you?" It was like old times . . . whenever her parents left the house.

Now, this hit standing by the van surprised Valerie, but it shouldn't have. Suddenly, Valerie heard him shout, "If you want to fight like a man you'll be hit like one! Stay out of my way!" *Valerie thought who was trying to fight except him? Clearly, he's confused.*

Mom waved her hand at Peter and Valerie to go inside. Theresa was standing on the hospital steps. Unfortunately, Valerie was too caught up in the moment to stop and greet her properly, as she should have. Valerie simply made a gesture and kept moving. They'd come this far and now it was time to see June.

Suddenly the tension in the air found its way to Valerie. Peter gave her a dirty look as they entered the hospital lobby. Valerie responded to it by screaming, "This isn't about you! Mom doesn't need this! Her daughter is in here fighting for her life! How dare you make this about you! You want to fight; then let's fight, but I'm going to fight back!" Mom started crying near the information booth and they both stopped in their tracks. That also happened to be when they noticed a couple of people just staring at the rowdy New Yorkers.

Ironically, Chuck wasn't going there with Peter. Rick, the resident family comic and warrior didn't want to come to blows either. Rick wouldn't shut up, but for once, he didn't want to fight. He just kept saying, "If you want to hit me, just hit me. I'll let you have that." That was the first recognizable sign that this incident was changing the family. Rick was growing up. Chuck was trying to hold on to his mother and the adults were crumbling at the seams.

They found out that June was located on the seventh floor and being taken care of in the Intensive Care Trauma Unit. As they approached her room, the couple from the lobby was leaving it crying hysterically. Their faces reflected horror. Initially, Valerie ignored the disturbing glimpses being displayed on their faces. *She thought, damn, we should have known better. They know June and we're acting out in front of them.* Valerie braced for the worst.

They went in immediately to see June and this person lying before them was not recognizable to Valerie. Her first honest internal reaction was one of relief. *She thought how do they know it's her?* Maybe it's not June, mix ups happen and for a second Valerie was privately joyous. Admittedly, that was an awful thought to have because if it were not June, it would have been someone else's sister, mother, daughter or niece. Valerie would have been ecstatic, in that moment, if it were another person. After staring at this individual for a while an uncomfortable familiarity began to rise. Valerie could kind of see it—June's face. June's features were emerging slowly and Valerie's brief gleam of hope was diminishing.

June was normally less than half Valerie's size. Now she laid before her about the same size or bigger, swollen from impact. Her eyes were bulging outward, just as Rick said. June's tongue was too big to fit in her mouth. Her faced looked bruised, there were rough scratches everywhere. There was also what looked like a hole located on the inner part of her left eye. June's hair was messy and she was hooked up to various machines. Valerie started to feel violently ill, so she quickly exited the room. Right outside the door was Theresa standing there staring at her in the most pitiful way.

Valerie asked, "How are you, Terry?"

She collapsed into Valerie's arms and said with a sound of relief, "It's good to see you, Val, all of you. I've been waiting a long time for y'all."

Time was moving slowly since this nightmare began. It already felt like they had been in Georgia for a week. Theresa told everyone that their presence helped her in the hospital. Previously, she felt alone because Rick and Chuck were running all over the place. Theresa was left alone quite often and was feeling it.

Suddenly, this kind looking man appeared and introduced himself as one of the resident chaplains. He said, "Hello, I'm Chaplain Anthony Marasin, but you can call me Anthony." The chaplain's presence immediately made a huge impact through his compassion and wonderful demeanor. His presence made a real difference; he was comforting and full of information, which Valerie found soothing.

Chaplain Marasin directed the family to a small sitting room that was located just outside of June's trauma ward. It was the perfect location because it enabled the family to stay close. Chaplain Marasin shared that he gained these helpful traits by working in a hospice. The unfortunate truth is, that was why he was so perfect for the job at hand . . . he was no stranger to saddened families or what seemed like the inevitable outcome lingering in the background.

No one knew why, but Theresa would be around one moment and then gone the next. She was often missing in action. Theresa was going through so many personal things now; it only compounded what was now going on with June. She lost her job, and the clock ran out on the eviction notice she received two months ago. Theresa was desperately looking for new employment and a reasonably priced apartment, all while checking in on June.

Also, while in the trauma unit, Theresa was called to the regular emergency room. An abusive ex-boyfriend that she had a restraining order against found out through a mutual friend that her sister was in the hospital. Theresa couldn't imagine why she was being called, but thought she should check it out. When she reached the emergency room and saw him, Theresa frantically began to back up and knocked over a cart. As it came crashing to the floor, she screamed, "Jim, how did you find me? Rick! Rick!" Jim grabbed Theresa's arms.

He said, "Don't run or I will fuck you up when I catch you."

A man in the ER saw the altercation and stepped in to help. He held Jim, who was screaming, "You don't understand! That's my wife! That's my wife! I love you, Theresa!"

She screamed, "I'm not his wife!" while running away.

The man in the ER was the only reason she was able to get away. In the past, Jim had made several pleas to make up, but Theresa just wanted to be left alone. She couldn't go back again. She remembers what Jim did to her every time she looked in the mirror. She pictured bruises that have come and gone. The truth is, Theresa was afraid to find out if their next reunion would result in her death. She had to leave him because Jim had threatened to kill her on many occasions. Now she wanted to get out of the hospital, have a cigarette and go home. Theresa settled for the cigarette. Theresa began stress eating and chain smoking. She felt a hole growing inside, an incessant emptiness that needed to be filled.

Peter could see Theresa's destructive behavior increasing and decided it had to stop. He always wanted siblings and got them. None were expendable. Peter took Theresa with him to a nearby drugstore to buy the patch. She had no intention of using it. Right now, food and cigarettes were her good friends and both were contending for the slot of best.

Valerie quickly became accustomed to rotating between June's bedside and what became known as the Peterson's sitting room. During rotation, she kept meeting new people; June had three jobs. Approaching June's room, she'd see lots of people. Once, Valerie saw a person so overwhelmingly hurt that she simply stood back and let her have a private moment. Her name was Janice Christopher.

Janice was a co-worker of June's, but felt like a family member. Valerie could feel her pain. Anyone could see and hear it. Janice made Valerie want to comfort her. A stream of tears hugged Janice's face while she shared how much she loved June. Janice replayed stories about their closeness. It was amazing. Not only was it good to know how others felt, things like these were a much needed temporary distraction.

Next was Brian Daniels. He was one of the first employers to come to the hospital. Mr. Daniels was a blessing in disguise. Valerie saw him lingering in the hallway and later found out that he knew June. He arranged for the Petersons to stay in a luxury apartment nearby, just in case they needed to rest or refresh. He and many others showed the Petersons that southern hospitality was alive and well.

It was also proof of the home June had built. A house isn't a home unless your heart is there. Pieces of June's heart were in New York, New Jersey, Maryland, and now Valerie could see it was also in Georgia. As the days went on, Valerie began to pair names and faces with stories June had told in the past. Memories of these conversations made Valerie feel as if June wasn't so far away.

Chapter 2

VALERIE was attempting to take in as much knowledge as possible. She wanted to learn all the science, as it related to June, even though she was waiting for a miracle. Valerie spoke to everyone along the corridor leading toward June's room trying to gather information. She was given business cards and forms, but nothing that really mattered. There wasn't anything that could disrupt her insatiable need to take it all in, except mom and Chuck.

They were the only two people who literally stopped Valerie in her tracks. The sight of either one of them brought a whole new level to this dreadful circumstance, by the nature of their title—mother and son. Valerie felt a responsibility to appear okay for them. She would look at mom and her thoughts would take over. *No mother should see her child this way. Mom created, molded and nurtured June into a beautiful young woman. Now she laid in front of her in turmoil. I couldn't imagine what mom was going through.*

Valerie remembered once a long time ago when her oldest daughter, Angel, slammed her finger in a car door and how much pain she was in because of it. Valerie could feel her own heart aching badly. She felt as if the incident might cause her to have a heart attack. Clearly, Angel was all right and Valerie knew it. There wasn't even a remote possibility of death. Yet, somehow it was apparent that Valerie was mortified.

Now, this thing with June is on the other end of the spectrum. Mom's child had a car slam into her . . . a car. June laid there before all of them, so obviously not okay. Death hovered around every inch of her room.

When mom walked into the room, June was no longer a sibling to Valerie, she became mom's baby girl. Being a mother made Valerie want to console mom wholeheartedly; from mother-to-mother. A different type of sadness would take over in her presence. *God bless mom as she looks at her baby hooked up to all these machines.* Acknowledging that mother daughter bond would shift Valerie's whole mentality. *How can I help mom? I can't give her June's well-being.* Mom's grim appearance reflected all that was happening. It seemed as if she was slowly being tortured and traumatized in every way.

Chuck, on the other hand seemed odd to Valerie. She couldn't put her finger on it at first, but he was just different. Already forever changed like everyone else. He was lost in a sick limbo between the unthinkable and a bad reality. Chuck was waiting for the adults who raised him to provide some strength. He wanted to trust and lean on them. He also needed to know they would step up if necessary. Chuck was being forced to grow up over night, although he was barely eighteen. Under the circumstance, he handled himself in an unbelievably good manner.

Sunday, Melody arrived from Maryland frantic to know about her sister's condition. Jan and Angel showed up as well. Valerie immediately pulled Jan to the side and asked, "What is my daughter doing here?" Her voice carried an under tone of anger as she continued, "she's supposed to be in New York with her little sister." The last time Valerie saw them was when she made a quick parental decision to leave her children in New York. As soon as she left, her last judgment as a parent was overturned.

Angel was now standing before her mother in Grady Hospital. There were many reasons that Valerie felt it was best Angel remain at home; the most important being Candy. She wanted her girls to stay in close proximity because she knew no one could support you like a sister. Valerie figured her girls would comfort each other in that unspoken way siblings do.

Melody was Valerie's unspoken sibling support throughout this fiasco. Melody seemed to always say the right thing. Sometimes even something Valerie had been thinking. It was Melody who ran all around the hospital with Valerie talking to police about criminal procedures and so forth.

Valerie gathered Melody, Jan, and Angel together. She said, "Brace yourself because it's really bad and she doesn't look good. It's hard to take." Right after the warning, Melody bolted to see June. Jan took a moment and Angel spoke with her mother privately.

Valerie said, "You don't have to leave the family room."

"But I have to go see her." Angel whined.

Valerie walked with Angel to see her Auntie Boo, as Angel often called June. Off to the side of June's door, they stopped. Valerie said, "Last chance, Angel. We can still turn around and go back."

Angel said, "I know it's bad, mom, but I have to see her. Please, mom."

"Okay, but you don't have to stay long. You can leave whenever you want. Remember that, okay baby?"

"Okay."

Angel's reaction resembled her mother's. Just as Valerie did, Angel stayed until she began to feel ill. Initially, both of them were so deeply disturbed by what they saw, it hurt them physically. Except, this time it hurt Valerie a little more standing with her daughter. Valerie took everything in more—the way mothers do when their child is present. Valerie's brain was suddenly being overworked because of mental post-it notes she was appropriately hanging for reference in later conversations.

Angel became sweaty. She felt dizzy and was rapidly elevated toward feeling faint. She had to leave the room and sit down. Angel tried to come back at other times, but couldn't take it. She talked herself into the room on one occasion while Valerie was with June. Angel watched the way her mom moved in the space around her sister. She looked like she was guarding June's body.

Valerie may have come across as protecting June, but in reality she was just watching everything and everyone. She wanted to know as new things unfolded. Valerie listened to what the doctors and nurses were saying to each other, especially as they departed. Once after a nurse left the room smiling, Valerie noticed that June was looking better. Every hour that passed, her body deflated. She appeared healthier. The family looked for other signs of progress.

Theresa was feeling ill and began to complain quite frequently. Her moaning kept increasing. Theresa announced that she might consider checking herself into the hospital. She kept repeating her intent with growing momentum. When it seemed likely, Valerie yelled, "Unless you're about to top what happened to June, nobody's coming to see you!" and walked away. That was the last she heard of it.

Valerie was upset that Angel was brought to Georgia. She couldn't address it properly because there was too much happening. Distress about Angel's trip became buried along with a list of other things.

Angel was prodded to leave New York with Jan, which she did, hesitantly. Jan asked, "Don't you want to be with your mother?"

"Yes, but what about Candy?"

"Candy is too young for all of this? Besides you can call home anytime you want."

Jan needed a travel companion and support. Angel tried to help, but didn't know how to deal with this situation. She was only fourteen, but did her best. Angel didn't want to leave Candy, but she needed to see her aunt.

Before Angel left, Candy screamed, "I'm so upset!" and began crying.

Angel said, "Please don't be mad." as tears filled her eyes.

"First mommy left and now you're going too, it's not fair! I want to go to Georgia."

"I know, Candy, I'm sorry."

"You're the only person who tells me what's going on."

Angel said, "I promise to tell you everything. All you have to do is ask. We will know more if I go. Don't worry, I'll tell you everything, even if Mommy doesn't."

"Ok."

Candy stopped crying, but she was still angry and didn't want to see Angel leave.

She wanted to be with her aunt too, but quickly made her peace with not going because it wasn't in her control. Candy was always great that way.

During 9/11, Valerie briefly struggled to find a reason for happiness to share with her children. She so desperately wanted them to be okay. Her fear was that she was affecting them negatively. The girls saw their mother numb, sleep deprived, angry, and simply afraid. They also watched her become fearful to ride the subway and cringing from the sound of every aircraft that passed.

They discussed various things candidly at the dinner table. September 11, 2001, swiftly, became the topic of choice. Valerie told them that as bad as it was, it could have easily been worse for them. While many lives were lost, she reminded them, their mother came home. She may have come back hurt and shaken, but she did come home. The girls always helped her look for the good side of things.

Six years later, on a very different subject, it was easier. It didn't make June's accident hurt any less, but Valerie was aware that it could have been worse. Chuck or someone else could have easily been inside June's totaled car, as well. The car could have been filled to its capacity, but it wasn't. June's vehicle could have rolled over after being impacted and hit numerous bystanders. The scenario could have played out a thousand times worse, but God is good every day.

Chapter 3

VALERIE first met Pastor Philips and his wife Ellen at June's housewarming two months before the accident. Ellen arrived at June's house extra early to help. Valerie could see that a wonderful sisterly chemistry existed between them and it was great. Valerie loved seeing that June had found an extended family.

Much later, in the midst of June's housewarming Valerie was sitting on a bar stool at the kitchen counter. There was a clear view from there to the dining room where June was sitting with her friends. Valerie was going to ask June if she would like some Caramel Cask & Cream because it was her favorite drink. It was as June put it, "A step up from my usual." June's usual being the regular Cask & Cream version.

Valerie had gotten into the habit of buying it for June whenever she visited. They had shared that drink countless times. They would drink a bottle and talk all night. Truth be told, Valerie preferred wine, but this was a way of bonding with June. Valerie wanted June to associate bliss with the time they shared.

Looking on from the kitchen, during the housewarming, Valerie noticed that June was elated. She was happier than Valerie had ever seen. Time was moving extraordinarily slow and Valerie was living this joyous moment at a snail's pace. June's smile was wide and filled with pure delight. Somehow time manipulated itself and allowed Valerie to really focus on June. Valerie had never experienced such a thing. It was wonderful and strange. June's sheer bliss was radiant. Joy bounced off of June and reflected onto Valerie. The air was filled with a miraculous gleam. Valerie could feel God's Spirit as golden specks dropped from the air like confetti. This unusual time warp was astounding, but when it was over that was it. No time had lapsed at all in Valerie's leisurely flash.

June had reached fullness and was living the dream. She had reached this place she had been searching for subconsciously. June finally found all that she had been looking for in Georgia. The family had never seen June this way.

Valerie was almost afraid to get up wondering about what just happened. That clairvoyant glimpse was priceless and she felt privileged to receive it. Angel walked in the kitchen and looked at her mother's weird expression and said, "Mom? Are you alright?"

"Yes baby." Valerie continued, "My sweet Angel, please go and ask your aunt if she would like a drink."

"Alright."

Valerie was still fixated, so she kept watching. Angel went into the dining room, leaned down and whispered in her aunt's ear. June turned her head toward Valerie, wide eyed and smiling. June shook her head affirmatively because she knew what was coming. Valerie took June her newly improved drink of choice and rubbed her back.

"Sit down, sister." June said with glee.

"No, no, enjoy. I'll see you later." Valerie left; not wanting to alter the moment in any other way because June, the family drifter, was settled.

Hours later, after everyone left, June and Valerie stayed up and spent time together. Valerie could see that June was exhausted, but she wouldn't go to sleep. "June, get some rest." Valerie urged.

"No, you're leaving in the morning. I'll stay here on the couch. Wanna watch a movie?"

Valerie sat on the floor next to the couch and said, "Sure. Why not?"

They watched the movie, *Roll Bounce,* but talked all the way through it. Valerie had never seen it before, but found it hysterical. She explained to June how it practically duplicated a time when she went skating with Jan every week. June thought she was kidding. Jan would have testified to the similarities had she been there. They would have to watch it all together one day.

Pastor and Mrs. Philips visited June in the hospital and prayed with the family. Everyone had been praying, but not as a unit. Pastor Philips spoke to the entire family saying, "Concentrate your efforts and be in agreement with each other." Pastor Philips preached, "We are asking for the miracle of a full recovery, Lord. Everyone lay your hands on our sister, June, and ask God repeatedly, for a full recovery. Do it together and as individuals." Pastor closed by saying, "We ask this together in agreement in Jesus' name. Amen."

Pastor Philips put the family on the right track. The Petersons did the best they could. They believed they were all in agreement, but they weren't. Due to love, they wanted the same thing, which was for June to be alive and well. They tried, but were not on one accord.

Some prayed for June's life. Some prayed for a quick and peaceful death, which they saw as inevitable—so that her pain would end. Others requested that God do what was best for June. All requests were understandable and even honorable, but still not a prayer in unison. A prayer in agreement must be clear and concise. Regardless of what was done, Pastor Philips delivered a glorious prayer and it helped. Valerie could see and feel an immediate difference among the whole family. Their spirits were lifted and they felt armed with the word of the Lord.

After Pastor Phillips and his wife left there was a knock on the door. It was a social worker, representing Shelly Christopherson—the woman who ran her car into June's.

"Hi. You're the Petersons, right? I'm Ms. Shelly Christopherson's assigned social worker and she asked me to let you know that she would like to meet the whole Peterson family, as well as visit June."

The vibe in the room quickly changed. Mom said, "No! No! No!" and began to weep but continued, "She cannot see my daughter, but you make sure and tell her to do better, so that this doesn't have to be in vain. She needs to turn her life around!"

Peter furiously interrupted, "I hope she goes straight to hell! Tell her that!"

Not one family member wanted Shelly to see June, although several wanted to go to Shelly's room. Valerie had a need to see Ms. Christopherson, this person who drastically altered all of their lives. Valerie wanted to stare into her eyes. Valerie wanted to know what she looked like. *Valerie kept thinking I guess we are all connected because this random stranger impacted my family tremendously.* She didn't want to talk to Shelly, but was compelled to go so she could remember her face.

Honestly, Valerie was curious as to what Ms. Christopherson might say. *What can be said to the family members of someone you have mowed down?* Valerie also wanted Ms. Christopherson to see her face and all the pain in it. Valerie hoped she'd always remember June and the pain she caused.

Melody, Valerie and Angel went to see Ms. Christopherson too. For Valerie it was as if her ears temporarily stopped working. She couldn't hear much of anything. Shelly's words flew into a black hole where Valerie repelled her sound. Upon Valerie's first glance, she noticed how easily Shelly sat up and moved while June was catatonic. Valerie was so distracted by it that she couldn't concentrate. She had never before been so aware of a person's movement. It was mesmerizing. As Shelly moved, Valerie's mind kept flashing back to June's lack of movement.

Valerie saw Shelly's lips moving, but remained in a trance not hearing what she said. Shelly held Melody's hand while speaking. It was a startling visual that helped knock Valerie out of her haze just in time to hear Melody deliver mom and Peter's messages; then offerings of forgiveness. Forgiveness was necessary to move onward from all the negativity. Valerie committed Shelly's face to memory. This single white, thirty-eight year old female who looked as if she were almost sixty, had blond hair and is now etched in Valerie's mind forever.

The mere sight of this woman made Angel tear. This was the first time Angel felt an intense amount of anger that she didn't let take full control. She had grown up. Angel was so angry, she wanted to strangle Ms. Christopherson, but she just stood back and cried silently. Angel said nothing, letting the adults take the lead. Later, she called Candy and gave her an update.

Valerie remained in an odd kind of stupor as they left. The further they got from Shelly the more livid she felt. Anger was building inside her and trying to take over. Valerie wanted to hate her, but that isn't who she is anymore. Valerie had only hated one person, but learned early in life that wasn't the way. She couldn't afford to hold on to the negative energy. It wasn't worth the self-inflicted trauma that comes with it. Besides, Valerie didn't want to wreak havoc on herself or anyone.

The day of the accident Officer Cosby told the Petersons about Ms. Christopherson. It was the first time they heard her name—Shelly Christopherson. When he said her name Valerie knew she would remember it forever. The name rang in Valerie's ears.

Officer Cosby said, "Shelly was under the influence of crystal-methadone when she climbed into her car. There was also a crack pipe inside her vehicle. She had been drinking heavily and her blood alcohol level was through the roof. Ms. Christopherson had no insurance and her license was revoked several months ago. You wanna know something else? She's done this before, three times to be exact."

"Well, why isn't she in jail?" Valerie asked.

"We've done all we could. Shelly managed to virtually escape the law every time."

Had this menace to society been handled appropriately in the preceding cases, June might be fine. The only difference to this offense was the person—June. Shelly had ten previous criminal charges against her and now the crimes she committed against June added four more.

Everyone was in the family room listening to the doctors describe June's state. Every other sentence was negative. Whenever the doctors spoke, one would open stating, "It is a safe assumption that June is brain dead, but with that said, this belief has not been declared because the medical definition of a brain death has not yet been fully met. When proclaiming a brain death, the person would have to fail all signs of life twice consecutively."

Then another would continue by saying, "Ms. Peterson was given this test repeatedly and would fail once, but not twice. She's not breathing on her own, but she is still breathing. Another time, a tube was removed from her throat and she coughed. It may seem like nothing, but coughing is a basic human reaction, which means . . . she's alive."

This was enough to give the Petersons hope. They had received many glorious miracles previously. A miracle should never be taken lightly, but what's one more? Valerie too had previously been in a major car accident. Her car was practically totaled. The frame had been compromised; all windows shattered, sections crushed and there was a hole that you could see through clearly.

Valerie's accident happened at the end of a great night. She and Jan had been out with friends. Valerie went to get the car making her way back to pick up Jan. As she began moving through a green light, a yellow cab driver on the adjoining street decided to go against the light seconds after her. The taxi raced forward at full force. Valerie saw the car approach fast and fierce out the corner of her right eye. Valerie braced for impact because it was imminent. The cab was moving so swiftly she wasn't able to evade it, although she gave it her best shot. Bam! Valerie's car was struck hard and was rotating high-speed through the street.

Valerie's car spun out of control rapidly toward a small scattering crowd on the sidewalk. She screamed, "God! Please don't let me hit the people!" Valerie didn't pay much attention to the enormous building behind them. She accepted that she would plunge into it. "Oh, Lord!"

she screamed and the car stopped. It screeched to an immediate halt without anything she could see stopping it. It was a visual phenomenon because of the brutal energy that propelled her car in the first place.

When the car came to a prompt standstill, Valerie hit her head on the steering wheel before being pulled back harshly by her seatbelt and fainting. Valerie regained consciousness while being pulled out of her car by strangers frantically mumbling about the liquid coming from the car. Her body ached all over. It was a scary inconvenience, but outside of that she was okay.

Valerie also experienced another type of car related miracle, years ago while driving the family back home from Georgia. It was a fourteen hour ride and she began to feel strange. Valerie was on the New Jersey Turnpike and noticed she was closing in on two huge trucks. She's no fan of driving alongside large vehicles, so she decided to change lanes. That's when Valerie realized that she couldn't move her legs. They were unbelievably heavy. Valerie struggled to shift, but her body appeared to be paralyzed from exhaustion. She was instantly afraid and continued to get dangerously close to the ongoing traffic. She glanced over her right shoulder and saw her children sleeping peacefully.

Valerie whispered, "Help me Father. Please let them stay asleep and help me." Out of nowhere, she felt strong hands take control. One firm hand lifted her right foot on and off the gas pedal as appropriate. Another swiftly maneuvered her left hand. The car was led to a rest stop parking lot. It came to a full stop and the gears shifted from drive into park. Valerie managed to get some rest and the children were none the wiser. She praised God all the way home.

Mom has also spoken about being in a car accident while pregnant with June. She said that it was so bad they received last rites as a result of it. Things were touch and go, but they made it. There have been many other things too like a massive fire that the family survived. Flames engulfed the whole premises and everything was lost except what was most important, their lives. As far as they were concerned, another miracle could surface any moment.

They listened for a miracle every time the doctors spoke. There were two physicians that would speak to the family; Doctors Gomez and Green. They were a great reminder of it's not what you say it's how you say it. Dr. Gomez would simply be factual, and the facts were against June. Dr. Green would also stick to the facts, but possessed the more desirable bedside manner. There was no way to make this a good situation, but his delivery provided a bit of breathing space.

Much of what June was going through seemed like a miracle and they fully expected more to manifest. She steadily kept doing well in small areas like her sudden ability to be off blood pressure medicine. Something June was previously unable to accomplish. The family was never given a good picture, but mentally, these small triumphs were adding up. Valerie thought that June would keep winning the little battles and eventually they would win the war. June's inability to fail the test twice was a sign of hope for a prayerful family that has faith in the Lord.

Prayers continued nonstop. Valerie would even stand by June's bed and pray both aloud and silently. She also told June to pray. "Speak to the Lord June. You don't need your mouth to talk to God," she said. Valerie told June how beautiful she looked. She was beautiful to her sister. In the end, I suppose, that's all that matters. That someone who loves you can look at you, no matter what's going on and say you are beautiful and really mean it. June's internal beauty was shining through her flesh.

Chaplain Marasin made the Petersons aware of the hospital chapel. They decided to attend a mass. The chapel was lovely. In the entrance there was a place for prayer requests and they filled that box to capacity. They prayed together as a family.

Two days after arriving in Atlanta, the family was still living out of the family room. The Petersons had been led to believe that this room was theirs as long as June was in such a bad condition. So they operated as such, viewing it as a God send. It was located on the seventh floor right outside of the double doors that led to June's unit. To be any closer would have meant to sleep in a hospital bed. It was perfect because it kept them close to June like they wanted. The hospital attendants kept others out and said let someone know if anyone bothered them.

The Petersons occupancy showed in a variety of ways. Someone placed a large folding table in the center of the floor. They also brought things to clean the room because no one had since they set up camp. They would even lock the door as they slept; waking up for updates about June.

A staff member mentioned that the Petersons should free the room up for a while. They should've realized it because the whole floor was filled with people and similar tales. There were families just like theirs who were sleeping exposed in hallways and waiting rooms everywhere. Their minds didn't let them acknowledge why they received obvious special treatment; they only focused on June.

Valerie approached an unfamiliar nurse, due to a new week and shift changes and asked, "Is there an available area in the hospital to stay?"

The nurse replied, "Normally, there would be. I would love to be of assistance, but the only room we have to offer is being occupied by some pushy New Yorkers who refuse to vacate. Besides, you don't want to be in there, that room is generally offered to families of patients about to die."

Valerie felt like dying when she said that. She probably should have told the nurse that she was one of those concrete jungle walking New Yorkers, but knew she would find out soon enough. Truth be told, the Petersons were not pushy. Had the issue been addressed properly, they would have never stayed in that room. It was simply a miscommunication that led to a misunderstanding.

No one realized they were given this "gift" because June was never expected to leave the hospital alive. The hospital staff thought she would die over the weekend, but it was now Monday. No staff member expected her to survive for as long as she did, but she lingered and fought. The Petersons left the family room, but couldn't bring themselves to fully leave the hospital. They stayed around, the hospital scattered among other people. Their locations kept changing, but the Petersons just couldn't leave.

Being removed from that particular area, the family began to discuss the option of taking June home. It was a great idea for some and not so great for others. Valerie did not agree with that suggestion. She didn't know if June was going to live or die, but she did feel any chance she had existed within these walls.

Valerie wanted to just grin and bear it and agree with the majority, but she couldn't. It was not June's time to go home. She needed to stay where the doctors could possibly assist her needs. She needed to be watched medically by the people who might be able to do something.

Chapter 4

TUESDAY, April 25, 2006, the Petersons took part in June's Last Rites ceremony. Valerie wished she had thought to call a priest when all of this began, not only for June, but for the family. June's Last Rites Ritual was performed by Father Mason of Atlanta's Sacred Heart Church. Fr. Mason demonstrated great compassion. He made an endlessly frustrating situation better. Immediately, Valerie felt more whole, they all did. That day, Fr. Mason catered to both June and the family. No sooner had the ceremony concluded; an unimaginable tranquility came over Valerie's mind. Serenity was hers. She immediately knew that everything was going to be alright.

Later that evening, Valerie noticed two new things about June's face. These things were disturbing. June's face had matured significantly. Finally, Valerie could see the resemblance to mom that everyone mentioned their entire lives. There was a split second of joy to have seen this wonderful familiar glance of connection at last, but it turned into a negative. It hurt Valerie to suddenly be able to picture mom lying in a hospital bed looking like what she could only describe as death. The other disquieting look Valerie had seen before on countless others in their caskets. June's new face was all too familiar. This unwanted, but recognizable emergence tried to send her mind to a place it was not yet ready to go. So, Valerie did the only thing that she could, which was to ignore it. At this point, she could not conceive what was so clearly obvious.

Valerie now realized that Peter had identified something earlier that she could not. There was a point when Peter came to Valerie and said ever so delicately, "People tend to feel a little better when everything is nicer. You should brush June's hair." Peter was right, but she couldn't do it. Valerie didn't think they should bother the area that had the issue. She thought the untidiness was justifiable, due to the massive head trauma and operations to alleviate swelling in her brain.

The doctors were always messing with June's head. After one procedure in particular, June came back to the room with some hair shaved. There was a tube lodged in that spot to drain fluid in hopes of taking some pressure off the brain. Things like that were necessary, but often made reentry into her room difficult. Another time when entering again, June's eyes were taped shut. Previously, her eyes had been open and blinking. Her eye movement was rather mechanical, and abruptly stopped without warning. The nurses explained that June's eyes were taped closed for preservation. That way they would be in perfect condition if she regained consciousness.

Valerie had been talking to her friend Gail, who suggested a handful of Bible verses to read. The only problem was that's when Valerie realized that she left her Bible in Brooklyn. Valerie rushed downstairs to the hospital gift store and purchased a small King James Version Bible. She used her new Bible for the rest of the night to assist in prayer for June. Valerie sat at the edge of June's bed, by her side patting her left foot that stuck out from underneath the sheets. With the continuous traffic in and out of the room, it seemed like the best place to be left uninterrupted. Valerie didn't think it mattered where she touched June, just that she did. She spent the rest of the night holding her sister's foot, praying and reading.

Valerie's spirit was at ease for a change. She went back to the apartment to wash and change clothes. Valerie recalled one of the doctors saying, "There isn't one broken bone in her body." That meant there will be one less hurdle when June gets out of the hospital. Valerie seemed to be looking back over these past few days quite a bit in her exhausted state which tired her further.

Valerie was mentally and physically worn down. These flash backs kept her awake for a time. She also thought about when she stood over June's bed singing, His Eye is on the Sparrow. That was the last thought she had before she fell asleep while waiting for her ride back to the hospital, which never came. Valerie did need the sleep, but she just wanted to be with June.

Part Two

The Worst Day

Chapter 5

ANGEL woke everyone up by yelling, "Hurry, we've got to go!"

Valerie didn't even know that anyone else was in the apartment until she heard her scream. Angel was lying down on the bed next to her mother, and at 8:30 a.m. sharp she jumped up petrified.

Angel screeched, "We've got to go! Hurry, hurry! Let's go to the hospital!" She stood there crying with tear streams adorning her cheeks.

Valerie said, "Calm down, its okay. Everything is going to be alright."

"Alright, but we've got to go." Angel replied. She stopped shouting, but went around the spacious room from person to person and begged them to move fast. She felt like something was wrong.

Valerie on the other hand felt great. She woke up feeling fabulously refreshed, and good. *Valerie thought things will get better today. I can feel it. My baby is just anxious to see her aunt. She'll see. Everything's going to be alright.* Valerie knew in her gut that everything would be okay. She fully expected to receive some favorable news regarding June's condition today. Peter drove everyone to the hospital.

When the Petersons arrived at the hospital they went to June's room immediately. It was different this time. The room and June struck all of Valerie's senses as odd. In fact, everything was unusual. June's room was serene and she looked peaceful, not at all like she was in the fight of her life.

For the first time, the entire staff was being overly kind. The expressions on their faces were strange; more focused and solemn. They were noticeably careful not to get in the family's way. Normally there would be nurses hustling and bustling around, or a doctor saying, "Please step out of the room for a moment while we test the patient." No nurse said, "Only two visitors in the room at a time."

June looked less traumatic. Her bed was nice and neat, which it hadn't been because of constant interruptions by staff. June's blankets were always ruffled. There were fewer wires attached to June too.

The staff was great but someone was usually annoyed because the Petersons never went away. They watched everything and Valerie watched, as well as questioned. She had always been naturally inquisitive. Knowledge tends to put her soul at ease. When Valerie's deeply troubled she asks way too many questions. The Petersons stayed in June's room together until they were led to a meeting room where the doctors were waiting.

Dr. Gomez said, "June Peterson was once again given the test for brain death and finally failed twice. She was declared dead at approximately 8:30 a.m. this morning."

Mom wailed immediately, which led a weeping symphony around the conference room table, among the Petersons, all except for Valerie. *Valerie thought oh God, the worst has actually happened. June died.* Valerie was surprised that she hadn't begun crying too especially since mom was tearful. Ever since she was little, the sight of mom crying made Valerie fall apart. Later in life, the beginning signs of mom's tears would get her started. The sight of her tears would send Valerie to a hurt place. Always wanting mom to be okay, the emotional display was often too much to bear. Now, Valerie sat there unable to cry.

Mom continued to weep and said, "Look at Jan, go to her."

Jan immediately said, "No, no, no." as she gestured her away.

Next, mom said, "Hold the children."

Valerie attempted to, but everyone needed their own private moment. Valerie then became frozen at that point in her own sorrow. Mom was still talking, but Valerie couldn't hear what she was saying.

Valerie felt like her heart was slowly drowning. A single tear began to fall from Valerie's left eye. Mom got up and walked toward Valerie with her arms extended for an embrace. *Valerie thought, thank God.* Mom held Valerie in her arms. The tear made its way down her face as Valerie focused hard on breathing.

Mom whispered, "Pull it together, they need you right now."

Valerie's tear dried up and the others retreated. June's death hit everyone hard, but Peter's pain seemed easiest to identify. Visually, he appeared to take it the hardest.

Right after the Petersons were given the news, Police Officer Sam Cosby came into the conference room. He talked about charges, evidence, and building a case against Ms. Christopherson. Officer Cosby said, "I need to take pictures now that Ms. Peterson has passed away. They'll be added to her case file. These photographs will be sent to the District Attorney's Office. I know the timing is bad, but this has to be done fast. You can be present if you like. That's up to each of you."

Valerie quickly said, "Yes."

"Well come on then. Follow me."

Valerie sat in the back of the hospital room while Officer Cosby maneuvered around June's hospital bed taking pictures from various angles. Once finished, Valerie went back to the conference room to be with her family.

Suddenly, at the worst possible time, everyone wanted to talk to the Petersons. They needed to be alone, but it was obvious that wasn't going to happen. The Petersons went from a conversation with the doctors, to the police and now with someone about organ donation. They were trying to process that June had died, not participate in the talk marathon that had been initiated.

The organ donation representative sat down and said, "June Peterson has remained on life support to maintain her organs. That is necessary in case you as a family decide organ donation is something you're interested in." She continued, "Only people who die a brain death qualify making actual organ donation somewhat rare. We don't mean to be insensitive, but that's why it's so important to ask when death occurs in this manner. So, how do you feel about donating Ms. Peterson's organs?"

There was total silence for a brief moment and then the room erupted. Almost everyone in the room seemed to want to say something, except Valerie. She honestly didn't think that was a conversation for everyone. In Valerie's mind, this decision belonged to either Chuck or mom and if they wanted further opinions they would ask for it. Valerie waited for mom to speak knowing Chuck wouldn't. When she did everyone became quiet.

Mom answered, "No. June has suffered enough and that's that. The answer is no."

The representative asked, "Are you sure?"

Mom tilted her head to the side and gave the young lady a half crazy look that screamed I will beat you, but said nothing. She was clear.

Then the representative said, "I understand. June will be taken off life support immediately. It's up to each of you whether you want to be in the room when that happens. Thank you for your time."

Theresa wasn't in the hospital. She had been dealing with the real possibility of homelessness, but suffered in silence. She might have been on the street when the family left town, but kept trying to handle her business quietly. Theresa was finally asked to see an apartment when she received a call from Melody about June.

Melody cried and said, "I'm sorry, Terry, but we lost her."

"No, no, no, Mel! She can't be gone." Theresa screamed.

"I know . . . we were told that June was gonna be removed from life support. If you want to be in the room, you better get over here."

Theresa said, "Alright, I'm on my way." and pushed her issues to the side and rushed to the hospital.

Angel didn't want to be in the room. She knew it would be too much. Angel wanted to call Candy, but didn't know what she would say. *I'll call her later, but I hope mommy speaks to her first.* Angel knew that Candy would want to be right there because they spoke about this very thing on the phone. Angel wanted Candy to get her wish, but this was no movie.

During that conversation Candy said, "I want to be able to say that I was there for Aunt June. Do you know what I mean?"

Angel said, "Yeah, but it's not as easy as you think. Mommy was right to want to leave us out of this. I don't know how I'm gonna get over all of this."

Candy continued, "I wanted our good bye to be like in it is in the movies. I wanted to sit next to Aunt June on her bed, as that high pitched tune blared and the vibrant line went flat. I wanted to talk to Aunt June and be one of the last people she saw. I wanted to make her feel loved and comforted leaving this world."

"That's a beautiful sentiment, Candy."

In the hospital, June's last worldly scene was nothing like that cinematic outlook. There was no faint chit chat being exchanged. June was not looking at them, but they believed she knew they were there. Even if she didn't, the personal discomfort was worth it because of the sheer possibility that June may have been aware of what was happening.

Valerie, Theresa and Rick went back to June's room and waited for them to remove the support. Theresa thought if June was ever going to breathe or do anything on her own, it was now. Theresa sat in a chair on the side of the bed, at June's right.

Rick was sitting at the foot of her hospital bed on a stool. He was in the room because he wanted to feel like they said good bye.

Valerie stood in the back off to Rick's right side. Valerie could see June's room filling with departed ancestors. There were more of them this time, many of whom she didn't recognize.

The nurses entered and proceeded to turn off the monitors and machines. The deceased loved ones hovered closely around the bed as though they were looking for something. One by one another machine was turned off, but when the breathing machine stopped it was impactful.

Valerie stared at June's chest intensely and it simply went down. It sunk further than she thought a chest could and never lifted again. A gorgeous illuminating multicolored light lifted away from June's body. The deceased family members smiled and focused on it as if they had hit the jackpot and just like that they disappeared. June was no longer in the building.

A nurse asked, "Would you like us to remove the mouth tube as well?"

Valerie nodded and said, "Yes, please. Remove everything."

The nurse continued. She removed and lifted the tape that was holding the tube down; revealing another hole. It was a literal opening not far from June's mouth that was not previously visible.

Valerie was numb until that point. Prior to that sighting, she had convinced herself that the car accident was so swift that June was instantly unconscious. It was a notion that made it possible to believe that June never felt pain. *Valerie took one look at that unnatural opening and thought there is no way that didn't hurt.* Valerie's face must have revealed this distasteful concept because Rick hugged her as she began to cry.

One of the nurses said, "Take all of the time you need." Then she left.

Truth be told, no amount of time felt right leaving June. They knew June was gone, but this now soulless body once housed a precious piece of their hearts. Valerie was not fully aware when everyone else left June's room, but suddenly she noticed she was alone. *Valerie thought this might be my last chance to touch my dear sister's body.*

Valerie didn't remember ever touching June much throughout their shared lifetime. It would happen on occasion during hellos and good-byes, but that was it. There were also one or two spontaneous, but scattered hugs in between, but not much. Now, standing before June's remains, Valerie felt compelled to embrace her body one last time.

Much earlier on in Valerie's life, mom spoke of touching a loved one after they had passed. Mom spoke so warmly and affectionately about the whole experience.

Valerie listened horrified. It seemed disgusting and she was appalled saying, "I would never touch a dead body. When it's over it's over."

Mom smiled at her with an odd gaze in her eyes, as if recalling something. She said, "You say that now because you're lucky enough not to have lost anyone really close to your heart."

As usual, she was right. Now, standing over June's body, all Valerie wanted to do was touch her while she still could. It was a strange feeling for her until she remembered what mom told her so long ago. Valerie also conjured up a conversation she had with her father, Chuck—whom everyone called dad. Dad was talking about how people would always touch his father's hair because it was so nice and wavy, but he never did, until he died. It was the first thing dad did when left alone in the room with his father's body.

Valerie didn't understand loss. Maybe something takes over because all of your personal guards are finally down. Or maybe, it's the mind's way of acknowledging you will no longer have access to this particular person. A physical connection is no longer possible, so you become obliged to initiate last contact. Here Valerie stood, touching June's face and recalling memories.

When Valerie was seventeen, a boyfriend of hers was sick in the hospital. Valerie didn't like how the hospital bed wouldn't allow her to really hug him. She jumped up over the railing that was put in place to enforce restrictions. She climbed into his hospital bed to fully embrace him. She lay in his bed with her head leaning on his shoulder as they watched television. Valerie stayed there just like that until a nurse came in and threatened to have her removed. Just as soon as the nurse would leave, she would leap over the bars and do it again.

Valerie longed to be young and impetuous as she stood over June's body. She wanted to climb up into June's bed and hug her, but didn't. She had been in the hospital for days now limiting how they touched. Although, Valerie would pat June often, she never fully hugged her because of the head injury. Valerie was always mindful of the situation. She didn't want to disturb June or risk hurting her further in any way. In Valerie's mind, she still didn't want to be bothersome. Valerie leaned over and gave June a heartfelt half hug, so as not to lift or upset her body.

Valerie outlined the bottom of June's chin with her finger. She then ran it from her neck down her arm, to her fingertips. One finger ran down her leg to her foot, which she held. The foot holding should have been a sign because she is not a foot person. This was the most she had ever touched June. One lifetime had passed and they could have filled it with hugs.

Valerie walked away from June and stared out the window. She turned and looked back. Valerie whispered, "I'm so happy for you" then screamed in anger, "but this fuckin' sucks for me!" At once, Valerie's body started to react to the emotion that seeped out in her statement. Valerie hadn't fully been able to let it out. So her body did.

Valerie began to cough violently. It was so uncontrollable that her body was jerking back and forth. She grabbed the sink in the room to maintain balance, but was afraid of hitting her head on it. Valerie began sweating profusely and while she didn't realize it at the time, she urinated a little and lost control of her bowels letting out a small amount of feces. Valerie's entire being cried for June, when she refused. When it finally stopped, she gathered the things in June's room. There were cards, stuffed animals, and a statue of an angel, several rosaries and prayer cards. She picked them all up, placed them in plastic bags and joined the family at the elevator banks.

As they waited for the elevator to arrive Valerie felt a personal loneliness like never before, steadily building inside. It was scary. This lonesomeness came quickly and it was deep. Valerie could tell this was the best it would feel and it was only the beginning.

Everyone attempted to help hold June's things, but Valerie wouldn't relinquish them. It was too soon. Valerie knew they weren't hers to keep, but she couldn't let them go right now either. She refused to hand over anything and started crying.

Valerie begged, "Please don't take them."

Angel grabbed her crying mother. "Its okay mom, no one's gonna take it away from you."

Valerie leaned on Angel's shoulder hard clutching June's things. She whispered in Angel's ear, "My sister's dead."

Valerie walked into the elevator defeated and in her child's arms. Angel held her up in a way that no child should have to grasp her mother. By the time they reached the ground floor, mom was holding Valerie.

"Mom, I'm all alone," Valerie murmured still crying as they walked through the hospital lobby.

Mom stopped, looked Valerie in the eyes and sternly said, "I assure you that is not true."

Words did not change how Valerie was feeling. She failed to receive the message mom was trying to give. Valerie didn't know what she should have, which is that she is never alone.

Valerie was one of the lucky ones having a huge family and good friends. Valerie didn't know how this underlying burden of loneliness grew inside, but it did. Maybe growing up with so many people and being the youngest left a wonderful impression that eventually became an Achilles' heel.

After leaving the hospital, they went back to the apartment to clear out their things before going to June's house. Valerie had no desire to go there. After all, what was the point? June wasn't there and wouldn't be coming home later. She would never walk across the threshold of her dream house again. *Valerie kept thinking why should I go there?*

Valerie reluctantly packed her bags and said something insignificant to Theresa who was sitting across the room. That's when it happened. Peter swooped down on Valerie.

He screamed, "I'm getting sick and tired of you!" as he punched her. Peter was always inappropriately dealing with his anger.

Valerie felt a blow to her body and screamed, "Why do you have to always make things worse?"

The sad truth was that today it didn't really bother Valerie. There was nothing else that anyone could do at that point, to make her feel any worse than she already did. She didn't need to hit rock bottom. Valerie was already laying far beneath it. She barely noticed that she wasn't even trying to tunnel a path back up from below.

She was unwittingly plunging further into a self-made grave. Peter's hit was simply one of the tools Valerie allowed to help push her further under the ground. As Peter swung at her, Valerie attempted to fight back, but everybody lunged in between them. Before they separated, Peter's long arms and legs allowed him to land a kick and a punch or two. The crowd pulled Peter into the hallway, but mom stayed inside.

Mom said, "You know how he is. I expect better from you!"

Valerie screamed repeatedly, "My sister died too! My sister died too!"

Jan entered the apartment as Valerie continued, "Everyone can just leave me the hell alone!" She sobbed and continued yelling, "My sister died too!" Valerie no longer wanted to be strong and was outside of herself. She couldn't even control what she was saying, but she didn't care—all was lost.

Jan ignored Valerie's statement and asked, "Do you want to go to the morgue? We can go and sit with her together."

Valerie screamed louder, "June is no longer here! That is not my sister! June left me! She's gone!"

It was then with that comment Valerie decided she needed to be left on her own; and they wanted to leave her alone for a little while. So they stepped out the door. It would have been better if someone swore to ignore Valerie and let her go through all of her emotions. Valerie wasn't herself and the world as she had always known it was gone. She wanted to take back those words, but her misery only allowed garbage to discharge. She was sorry for taking her grief out on them, especially mom. Valerie didn't want to inflict or receive any more pain.

Mom was standing next to Angel in the hallway when she said, "She's gone crazy! We're all going crazy! It's just a matter of time and who's next. Brace yourselves."

Angel couldn't believe her mother had been screaming like that. *Everything has changed and not for the better.* She cried. Angel was worried. She felt like she couldn't lean on her mother during this ordeal. So she adjusted her behavior and tried to comfort her mother. Angel realized things were spinning out of control. *She thought mom won't ever be the same.*

Valerie could see how everything escalated to the point of her spewing those awful words. Why didn't she have enough control and compassion in the moment? She had just been beaten down by the news of June's death at the hospital, but they all had. The idea that June might have been in pain lingered on in the back of her mind. Loneliness struck again, hard. Valerie kept reassessing what happened.

The pain was taking on a life of its own. First Peter's pain literally rammed into Valerie confirming she was alone. Then her pain lashed out in the form of a verbal assault being launched. Who was next?

Angel entered the apartment next because Valerie had quickly become the family project. Angel said, "We don't have to go mommy. We can stay here together."

"No, baby. I need to be alone. I'm sorry." Valerie said as she kissed her daughter's forehead. She continued, "Please leave and go with mom. I'll be okay, I promise."

"Alright, won't you come too?" Angel pleaded.

Valerie thought about going with the family for Angel, but knew the answer had to be no. She needed to be left to deal with her pain. It took some time, but eventually the family agreed to go.

Valerie called Samantha because she was enraged by everything that happened. Valerie inquired, "Did anyone call you?"

Samantha said, "Yeah, I know. Peter called me right after the doctors told y'all. I just can't believe it. How are you holding up?"

"Long story, but I've got to get out of Georgia. I've spent almost all of my money down here and I need you to fly me back to New York. I'll pay you back."

Samantha said, "Whatever you need, but you do know you should stay, right? I'm sorry Val, but I gotta go. I love you. I'll call you again later." Samantha had been busy looking after everyone and trying her best to do what mom usually did.

Valerie understood, but she needed more today. Valerie quickly realized that she should have let someone stay. Samantha called Valerie back on her cell phone.

Valerie said, "Thank God, you called back, Sam."

"It's not about that, Candy is really upset and wants to talk to you."

Valerie braced herself to be the mother she hadn't been since she left New York and waited for Candy.

Candy said, "Hi mommy."

"Hi."

"I feel like I know what is going on but, no one's telling me anything. Aunt Samantha has been acting really strange today."

Valerie asked, "What do you mean? How has she been acting?"

"Way nicer than usual. She's trying to act happy, but I can tell she's sad." Candy continued explaining, "She looks like she lost her best friend and is acting really weird. Please tell me what's going on mommy."

Valerie answered any and every question that Candy presented. They spoke for a while, but Valerie started with what she knew Candy was asking about—June's death. Valerie sighed and said, "I'm sorry, baby, your Aunt June died today."

Candy's response was shocking, she said, "I knew she died. I was feeling strange all morning."

Candy thought June died before she left for school that morning, but no one verified what she was thinking. She was in class and her teacher called on her to answer a question. She gave a quick and silly answer. That's something Candy never did because she was always serious about her schoolwork. The teacher made Candy come up to her desk and asked her what was wrong. Candy became overwhelmed and started crying.

Candy said, "My aunt is dead," then she fainted.

The teacher took Candy to the nurse's office and called home. Samantha picked Candy up from school after that incident and took her home, but said nothing about June.

After that happened, Candy wanted to stay home and was allowed. She was worried about being kept out of the loop. She figured she would learn more listening to the adults at home.

Candy didn't return to school until almost two weeks later. It was for the best. After hearing about June, later that night, Candy became agitated. The only other time that Candy felt so bothered was a week or two before June's accident. She was having a series of vivid nightmares about death. She wasn't the only one who experienced strange occurrences in the family either.

Three weeks prior to June's accident, Valerie had an episode of her own. Previously, Valerie had taken a break from attending church. She planned to return, but hadn't. It was the middle of the week and suddenly, Valerie had an overwhelming urge to go to service right then. She couldn't believe how intense this feeling was to attend. The pull was great, so Valerie got dressed quickly and left the house. There was one obstacle after another, but she refused to be deterred.

Once Valerie reached church, she sat down without delay. Mass had already started and she was trying to receive "the word." Valerie was listening to the priest, but couldn't hear him. She'd never had this problem before, so she moved forward a couple of pews, but still heard nothing, but mumblings. Valerie sat up and struggled even more to pay attention. She was here for a reason, so she leaned forward determined to hear the priest. Instead of the priest, Valerie heard another speaking over him.

The voice had a tranquil sound. It said, "Something will happen in not one, not two, but three weeks." The voice clearly didn't belong to the priest.

Valerie looked around bewildered, but no one else seemed phased. One man sitting next to her looked unnerved that she was so frazzled. When Valerie calmed down and sat back, the word sister began to hang in the air in front of her face. Many other words followed, but they were spoken in the same angelic tone in a swift manner. Valerie caught a few words like accident and peace while sister just lingered. The voice seemed to be speaking faster than Valerie could comprehend. She began crying.

As Valerie wiped her tears, the voice said, "Your tears are holy. Do not worry. Everything will be alright. You will be alright. All is well as long as you don't listen to him." As quickly as it began, it ended.

Valerie didn't understand what had just happened, but she left the church unsettled. She didn't' even know why she had been crying. She felt like her spirit processed something that she was not fully able to know and the message was fleeting. She experienced this like one of those dreams you struggle to remember, but just can't. Valerie came home with a desire to check on her sisters and move to Georgia. Something she has never really wanted. Theresa was on her mind the most, but she called June.

"Hey, June! Guess what?"

"What?" June said.

Valerie said, "I'm finally thinking about moving to Georgia."

Valerie was excited and although June had always wanted her to move, June's response was, "Don't rush, Val. I'll help you make plans to do it right."

Valerie discussed moving with her children. Angel, who never wanted to even consider moving out of New York, wanted to pick up and leave immediately. Angel couldn't figure out what had gotten into them.

Two weeks later, Valerie dreamt that a loved one was hit by a car and was stuck on the side of the road. She couldn't see the person's face, but knew it was a female. In the dream, Valerie didn't know where this person was and couldn't get to her in time. She woke up devastated.

June was being thorough in planning her sister's move so it was going slowly. She died before the plans were complete.

One night, Angel said, "We should have gone to Georgia, mom. Maybe we could have stopped it."

Valerie didn't believe that. The warning was saying don't lose yourself in the negativity to come. It has the potential to be your end, but it should not be. It isn't your time yet.

Chapter 6

LATER, Valerie called her daughters' father, Charles. Valerie and Charles were never good with each other. They didn't work as a couple in any way, but Charles always knew how to lift her spirits. Charles was always good at making Valerie feel better when things were bad. Valerie wanted to be soothed and needed Charles to comfort his children. When she told him June passed away he was silent.

Valerie quickly said, "I'll call you back, Charles" but had no intention of doing so because she was frantically searching for help. That was the second time that Charles let her down during the crisis.

The first time was during a food break while June was still alive. Jan and Valerie were in a fast food joint and Valerie was on her cell phone. She told Charles about June and how she jumped on a plane to be at her sister's side. At the time, Valerie was still hopeful that June might live.

She said, "I left our children in New York because the situation is serious. I was too uncertain if what I'd find was appropriate for the girls. So I left them."

He asked, "When are you coming back?"

"I don't know when or if I'm coming back. I need to find out what's going on with June. She may need help. I might send for the children a little later, but not now. That's why I need you to step up and be there for them. Call them often, please go see them, pick them up and spend time with them. Their aunt might be dying Charles and their mother left. Samantha, Jan, and my father are with them, but they are not their parent. Let them know you're there too. Okay?"

The truth is that Valerie had to be with June in Atlanta. In her head, she'd secretly been a doctor for years, so what do you do in an emergency? Set up triage and that's what she did. In triage you quickly prioritize and help the one that needs you most. Only her supposed medical mind was failing her due to her heart's own agony. That's why doctors don't work on relatives. Instead of staying with who needed her most, she worked in reverse. Valerie clung to who she needed most at this time—June.

Valerie had to know how well June was doing. She had to hear June's status first-hand. She couldn't risk misunderstood translations. She couldn't even consider leaving Georgia until knowing June would be alright. At this point, Valerie could not fathom what was next. In fact, for her there was nothing next without June. Valerie had to remain in Atlanta for as long as it took. She would not have been able to breathe elsewhere.

After explaining the situation to Charles, while standing inside the worst fast-food place she had ever seen, Valerie begged him to check in on the girls. Charles hadn't been the most accountable father, but it would make a big difference. Charles told Valerie not to worry about them, but he was unable to visit them.

Valerie shouldn't have been shocked, but she was. She assumed that he would react differently due to the severity of June's condition, but was wrong. He had shown her who he was before and she should have believed him.

It wasn't Charles' responsibility to console Valerie, but when he couldn't supply even one word to temporarily supply comfort, she felt worse and more alone. Valerie sat there, still, in the chair crying and praying. She needed someone. Valerie begged God to send her someone. She needed to be sustained because she had backed herself into a dangerous corner. Outside of associates from work and mutual family acquaintances, none of her friends knew anything was happening. She hadn't told anyone. Valerie didn't want it to be real.

She cried, "I need help, Lord!" and the phone rang. Valerie picked up her cell phone swiftly without looking at the caller's identification on the screen and it was her good friend Gail.

Gail was brief and to the point, but all her words seemed to be heaven sent. She listened and also convinced Valerie to stay in Georgia.

She said, "I know it's an awful time, but it is also a significant time-frame that you will not be able to get back. I know that staying feels pointless because June is no longer around, but I urge you to continue to be strong." Gail continued, "You need to stay and be there for your family." She paused and then said, "You also need to stay and be there for yourself. I wish I could be there to help you through this." She had done enough.

Gail was with Valerie frequently through those days. She would talk to her on the phone or text Valerie and contribute brief moments filled with peace of mind and scripture. Gail was even involved in some of the private conversations Valerie had with June in her hospital room. Gail would speak wonderful words to June through the speakerphone. They often spoke this way. Once while speaking, Gail's brother, Lem interrupted their discussion and offered his condolences to the family during a three-way call. Lem's disruptions continued to increase and before long Valerie was talking to him alone.

Although Valerie and Lem had never met, Lem always offered her intense support, which allowed her to feel like they'd known each other forever. He was persistent about reaching out to Valerie because he and Gail were overly familiar with family loss, involving a sister. Lem's ability to make Valerie feel good during this needy time permitted her to develop a crush on him; sight unseen. Valerie had only done that once before when she was a young teenager. The face-to-face connection was nonexistent. Valerie vowed to never become attached to anyone else without meeting them first and gauging their chemistry together. Yet, here she was falling fast and hard for a guy she never met.

Gail continued to check in on Valerie daily, but she worked two jobs and attended college. She was happy when Lem started picking up some of the slack. It was alright because Lem was more than happy to do it. He called Valerie night and day and she loved it. Somehow the exchanges held her together for a while no matter how long they were on the phone.

Valerie wished June could meet Lem. June was good at spotting good friends and people for Valerie, but she wouldn't have wanted her to date Lem. Besides, Valerie could tell from their frequently raw and truth-filled talks that Lem wasn't the type of man she wanted. Lem had a ghetto appeal and was loud and boisterous. He also had some great qualities that Valerie considered a blessing.

Valerie told June how she couldn't stop thinking about this guy she only knew through telephone conversations. She was becoming obsessed with meeting him, but didn't think she should. Lem was somehow filling an ever growing void.

Part Three

Struggles

Chapter 7

BEING in the apartment alone was when Valerie first realized she was experiencing a serious struggle. At first, she was unable to identify exactly what was happening. Sometimes it was belief vs. desperate desire, good vs. evil, or the world vs. the afterworld. Then there were other moments when Valerie was experiencing denial vs. reality. These feelings would surface and resurface. Valerie failed to recognize that she was trying to feel whole, but nothing made her complete. She was unable to fill the "June Hole."

Utter misery hit again. It was worse this time. Valerie suffered from all of the same things, except now there appeared to be more depth to them. These feelings were unlike anything she had ever felt. Valerie was engulfed in pain, literally sitting in the midst of it and couldn't see anything else. Her feelings were deep, dark and clearly becoming destructive. As the seconds passed, she could feel this unique pain growing quick and fierce. They were demonstrating an unbelievable supernatural strength. This raw negative intensity was demanding that Valerie morph into someone or something new. These emotions felt like they had come alive. They were no longer part of what Valerie was feeling, but a separate entity burning her inside and assisting the hurt. When she rapidly reached an unbearable level of pain, she began crying again, violently.

Valerie was convulsing and choking. Her skin was extremely hot and felt like it might actually be on fire. The heat was painful to her skin and intensifying. Valerie surrendered to the agony without acknowledging that she had, but it was a fact. She screeched awful unnatural sounds at the top of her lungs. These unrecognizable squeals upset her ears. Valerie cried and screamed so much that she eventually ran out of tears. She should have known to stop then, but didn't.

Valerie's face swelled and her voice became hoarse. She continued to choke and it was obstructing her breathing, but she didn't care. Valerie's stomach started trying to throw things up, although it didn't work because she hadn't eaten much. Vomit kept trying to force its way up, sometimes releasing fluid. It was the gagging reflex that finally got Valerie up off the floor she had been laying on for hours.

When Valerie finally got up off the floor she ran to the bathroom sink and bent over it. She began splashing water on her face with one hand and tried to balance against the sink with the other one. She had been cut so emotionally deep that the wound was affecting her essence. It was as if she was being invaded. This intrusive emotional attack along with its physical ramifications on Valerie's body kept making an effort to urge her into insanity.

Valerie's body began to shake violently. She struggled to contain it. Valerie could feel the tension building and crawling underneath her skin. It was like hate was taking over her body. This "thing" wanted her to flip out again and was too strong to fight. More likely, Valerie was too weak. Her body convulsed harder. It was so bad at times that Valerie was worried she might hit her head. This is when she realized that people could actually make themselves sick. Ironically, Valerie was too sick to care.

Jan entered the apartment. She found Valerie in the bathroom and said, "Valerie, are you okay?" Her voice was incredibly gentle.

Valerie cried all her responses hysterically, "No!"

"Do you need anything?" Jan asked.

She screeched, "I need June!"

"Can I get you anything?"

"Get me June! I want June!" Valerie's screams were continuous.

Her whole body was aching, every inch of it, especially her heart. Its natural internal pounding had been replaced by an erratic throbbing. It was astonishing. Valerie's purely emotional state had beckoned her physical body to react at an intense level that words could not express. Valerie's mind was indeed altering her bodily state. She wasn't listening to Jan. Valerie wanted her to go away. She would have told her, but every time Valerie spoke, she hurt more.

Valerie had not even slowed down long enough to be still and listen for God. Her body was manic. This exaggerated energy she was experiencing would have been beautiful had it not been based in pessimism. This was pure electricity based in a corporeal structure. Valerie never thought God was far from her, but at this particular point, she attempted to push Him further than He had ever been. The enemy knew it and was trying to secure his footing in her weakness.

Jan, Valerie's niece, whom she always wanted to look after, was protecting Valerie from what she was unwittingly travelling toward. Jan was saving Valerie's life. She was also the girl that Valerie would fight for because of how someone treated her back in the day. Jan, the family drama queen took care of Valerie and was handling her drama. She rose to the occasion. The devil was talking to Valerie and she didn't realize it at the time, but she was listening. That was the night that her wrist never looked so good.

Valerie was bent over at the sink with Jan using a washcloth to cool her forehead. She was still gagging and holding the sink with her head slanted to the right. Valerie heard a voice that was not hers inside of her head whisper, "*Look.*" That's all it said, one word, but it was enough. The voice was warm, comforting and beautiful. It made Valerie want to gaze upon what it spoke of without more words. At first, her sight was blurry from all the tears she cried, so Valerie couldn't see, but she tried hard.

There it was again, except this strange voice lingered longer saying, "*Look.*" She tried harder to see. Valerie was able to focus for maybe two seconds and found she was staring at her wrist. This unfamiliar voice said, "*Yes*" as her eyes were transfixed on the prize. It may have been a millisecond but Valerie noticed that her body felt good and warm while vibrating from the yes. Nothing else was said, but she knew what it wanted her to do. Valerie felt confusion. The following words rolled before her eyes: One slit and all your pain goes away. You could see your sister. Valerie recognized that to be an evil lie. The devil was riding the wave of her misery. That's why evil is the majority of his name. Wickedness was attempting to reach Valerie at her weakest, but she couldn't give in to it.

Sadly, God was the farthest thing from Valerie's mind leaning over that sink. She allowed herself to be distracted so she couldn't seek Him, although, she so desperately needed Him. Mercifully, He came to her side. God shielded Valerie with special amour. She didn't know exactly when the voice's appeal lagged but Valerie did know it was during Jan's sink side speech displaying her unique ability to ensure her that she was not alone.

Valerie began mumbling, "He that is in me is stronger than he that is in the world."

Her like-a-sister, actual sister Jan kept talking, and the words were reaching Valerie on a subconscious level.

The last thing Valerie heard from Jan was, "I have you." and she did.

Previously in Valerie's life, she wondered what kind of pain a person could be in to subject themselves to personal torment; leaving them to believe suicide is the only way. Well, the war in Valerie's mind moved her closer to such knowledge. She was violently struck by overwhelming emotions in the situation. The worst part of this whole thing is that she was putting herself through the anguish. It's dangerous to feel option-less. Alone, Valerie couldn't see a way out of her pain.

Jan helped her to get off the fast track to nowhere, slow down and re-examine things. She had Jan. Valerie's much needed help was standing next to her readily available.

Generally speaking Valerie was always anchored in God. She would cry out for Him in love, but this time she cried out in fear. Valerie didn't realize it then, but she became temporarily disabled by the inconceivable depth of her own fears. Willingly, yet subconsciously thrown out of her holy place. The devil was using Valerie's fear to move closer.

Previously, Valerie thought that fear was a gift from God, but no longer. Too many evil things have tried to build a bridge on her fears to be linked to the Omniscient It was in between her fears that He put Valerie in check long enough to receive further assistance through Jan. Valerie could smell her own terror, which horrified her more. Her destruction felt imminent and real. Valerie didn't want to be weak. She wanted to be strong, but she was afraid. Luckily, she paused in perfect time to hear Jan.

No one else could have calmed Valerie like Jan. She was the only person who grew up with June and her. Jan was the only one who lived the same life with them, one moment at a time. The three of them shared many things together. "JuneJanValerie" rang in the background of Valerie's mind as Jan spoke to her softly. Valerie thought about how June served as maid of honor in both Jan and her weddings. Jan made her feel closer to June. While one definitely could not replace the other, Jan was probably the closest person to maybe understanding how Valerie was feeling.

God sent Valerie the right person. From childhood, all Valerie heard was, "JuneJanValerie! JuneJanValerie!" mom would call, June, Jan and Valerie as if they were one person. Growing up in such a close circle forges an unbelievable bond.

"JuneJanValerie!" mom would say it as if it were one word. It had a ring to it and it definitely had a nice sound to Valerie. It meant mom wanted them and she was the best; still is. As far back as Valerie could remember the tiny trio was always together and loved it. They had friends, but didn't need them because they had each other. They were happy children and were always being wonderfully creative. They played board games and made up things. When they weren't playing, they were singing and dancing. The list of performances ran the gambit from weddings to their favorite production, *The Wiz*.

Before Jan left, she made Valerie feel like she would be all right. Valerie would survive the night, something she wasn't sure of before Jan showed up. Valerie lay upside down on the couch, her head hanging over the side, staring out, but not really looking at anything. She only straightened up when she heard a minister's words piercing her soul through the television set.

It was the first time Valerie thought of God that night beside when making her desperate pleas. She had been able to block out the television prior to this program, but that was no longer the case. Valerie needed to listen and was compelled to do so. She was fixated on this program. She asked God to send her help and it turned up whenever she needed it, continuously throughout the night.

Eventually, Valerie was sitting fully upright, making and receiving phone calls. She felt normal again for a small period of time. Valerie spoke to some family members and a couple of close friends, for the first time since this tragic episode began. She knew she should have before, but that would have made it too real. Calls would have made it seem like what it was and Valerie wasn't ready for that reality. In fact, most people Valerie heard from were mutual friends of hers and Jan's. Valerie also spoke to co-workers. They knew because Saturday when all this began, she called her job.

The Saturday this incident started, Valerie called the insurance company where she worked. Mrs. Brown, the morning weekend receptionist, answered the phone. Mrs. Brown said, "Health Incorporated, this is Mrs. Brown speaking, how may . . ."

Valerie interjected, "Mrs. Brown this is Valerie Peterson. Can I speak to Mr. Johnston?"

Mrs. Brown replied, "He's not here. How are"

Valerie interrupted again, "How about Mr. Klein?"

"He's not . . ."

"Mr. Megs?"

"Valerie, they are all not here! It's a Saturday!" Mrs. Brown exclaimed, agitated because Valerie was usually so nice.

Valerie didn't mean to be rude, but kept cutting into Mrs. Brown's sentences because time was not on her side. She had to leave for Georgia.

"Mrs. Brown, please take a message. Tell them all that my sister has been in a really bad car accident and they need the family there in the hospital to make decisions. So, I'm going to Atlanta right now and I don't know when I'm coming back yet, but I'll call as soon as I can."

"I'm sorry to hear that Valerie." Mrs. Brown said somberly, "I hope . . . ."

"Did you get all of that?" Valerie inquired hoping that she didn't have to repeat it.

"Yes." Mrs. Brown answered, as if she finally understood.

"Good, thank you, I'll be in touch." Valerie said, just as quick and hung up.

Later on during Valerie's worst day, she also spoke to Samantha and Candy. They sent her silly pictures. Valerie returned an awful looking one of herself to them. She looked like hell. Valerie didn't know what message her picture sent, but theirs helped her mood.

That night, Gail called back to check on her friend. She literally talked to Valerie all night. They talked about everything and nothing at all.

Gail said, "You're doing amazingly well, even better than you realize." She continued, "In the end of this ordeal when you're finally finished grieving, you'll be armed with holiness. It's just a matter of how it will show itself."

Mom said, "Laying in the bed of a person you've lost can help." Valerie kept recalling things mom said about loss and wondered if that would be true for her too. *Could that make me feel better? Or is that just mom's way?* Valerie found herself wishing that she was in June's bed as she fell asleep. Then, hours later Valerie woke up to her cell phone ringing. It was a wakeup call from Gail. They developed a stronger friendship over the next few weeks; this support helped her remain functional. Their friendship focused Valerie and made her strong both mentally and spiritually.

Leaning over the sink, hearing that voice in her head caused Valerie to ask herself, "Was I suicidal?" *No, I couldn't have been.* She didn't want to believe it. The very possibility was the worst thing in the world to her. Realistically, it was necessary to examine the likelihood of reliving this disparaging scenario. Suicide is something that Valerie never imagined she would have to deal with in any form, but she was wrong.

Staring at her wrist, Valerie wasn't focused on not living. She didn't want to die. The full thought never really crossed her mind. Valerie wasn't even thinking about her sister on some level, she knew June was okay. Her destruction was being brought on because of not knowing. What did June's death mean for her life? Valerie was lost in her selfishness. She felt unbelievably alone, like she wouldn't be alright again. Everything hurt, both inside and out. Internally Valerie was experiencing an incommunicable ache that wouldn't go away. She was painfully and continuously uncomfortable in her own skin, to put it mildly.

Valerie didn't want to die. She was just no longer fond of waking up. She realized now more than ever that every new day is precious, but it was also a new day that existed without June. It was for this reason that Valerie wanted no part of it. June had always been a part of her everyday life, regardless of whether she wanted her to or not. The simple fact is there was never a time before that Valerie existed without June. She wasn't looking forward to finding out what time and space would be like without her. The unknown was unbearable.

Valerie wanted to stay asleep because June was now living full time in the midst of her dreams. In fact, the worst part about the grieving process for her was dealing with June's death daily. Valerie was in a special kind of denial because she was very aware of what was happening, but honestly kept waiting to wake up from the horror. She just wanted to escape from the nightmare of June's death.

Eventually, Valerie stopped waiting to get up out of this new reality. She was sleeping so much her worlds were crossing. When Valerie was awake, she wanted to believe she was asleep. When Valerie was asleep, she forced herself to believe she was awake. Valerie's mind was slowly trying to cope with the whole thing. Even in her dreams she was very much aware that June was no longer alive, but she was still there. That was all that mattered. June was visible in this dreamland. So Valerie embraced and loved it. Her dreams consisted of everyday life and June was always present, but she never spoke. This annoyed Valerie at first, but she learned to live with it.

There was only one dream that June seemed to be trying to communicate. It started with Valerie entering the family dining room. The rest of the family was in the kitchen. There was a couch in the dining area that wasn't normally there, and June was lying on it. Valerie was surprised to see her, but ecstatic. She knew that June had moved on into the next phase of life.

In the dream, Valerie felt like she finally lost her mind. She ran past June to the family in the kitchen.

She gleefully screamed, "Can you see her? June looks great! Can all of you see June?"

They said, "No."

Everyone shook their heads while looking at Valerie as if she were crazy.

Valerie ran back to June and sat next to her on the couch. June was gesturing with her hands wildly, smiling and sucking her thumb. Valerie knew she was trying to tell her something big but she couldn't figure out the message. June used to suck her thumb all the time when they were younger. That was the last time June attempted communication with Valerie. It wasn't, however, the last time she debuted in a dream.

Most of Valerie's dreams that housed June continued to be ordinary. In some, Valerie would be in her room alone putting clothes away and June would be sitting on the bed watching. Valerie would see June and speak, but she would become visibly distressed and not answer. Valerie stopped initiating conversation.

In other dreams, friends or family might be gathered around in the living room and she would be in the mix sitting on the floor or standing off to the side. June always looked as though she was a part of everything and seemed to be paying attention to what was being said; nodding or affirming.

Eventually, in the dreams, June trained Valerie to notice her, but not react. Valerie always wanted to talk, but June would never attempt to say anything, except for once.

Once, Valerie caught a really bad cold and quickly became very ill. She thought it was a simple case of the flu but her health continued to rapidly decline in a way that she never before experienced. Each day that passed, another part of her body ached and nothing seemed to help. Valerie's head felt like it was going to literally explode and she couldn't stop crying. Mom begged her to go to the hospital. Valerie could barely move and felt like she was under attack. It hurt to be mobile. Valerie kept laying down and would fall in and out of sleep. Each time Valerie slept, it felt like a deeper slumber. And the deeper it would get the more she would think of and see June.

At first, June held true to her previous dream form and just sat with Valerie. In the dream, Valerie was sick, resting in bed and watching June. Even though it was just a dream, seeing June always made Valerie happy. The further Valerie sank into her bed she began to feel like she was sleeping her life away. Valerie felt like she was dying.

When Valerie became aware of this thought, June started to say something. It might not have meant anything, but Valerie did not want to hear one word. The idea of the oncoming words gave Valerie a bad feeling. She immediately asked June not to speak and to go away.

When June disappeared, she woke up, instantly. Valerie used the limited strength she had to get up and practically crawl downstairs. In all of her pain, Valerie walked into the living room and made a point of sitting up. Valerie told mom that she would go to the hospital tomorrow, but now was time for prayer.

Normally, Valerie would read her Bible and pray every day, but she realized that being sick had distracted her from it. Mom prayed with her for hours. Valerie asked everyone who entered the room that night to pray with her and read Psalm 91. Each time a new family member read Valerie, felt better. By the morning, there was no trace of any ailment. She should have been praying more during this time, not less.

Another reason waking up became so taxing for Valerie was she no longer liked how she looked in the morning. June's death aged her significantly. Very early on, Valerie developed the very bad habit of crying in her sleep. She would often wake up with her face looking tear streaked, puffy, and beaten. Although, Valerie became accustomed to this distorted face, she didn't want to embrace it. Valerie also developed gray hairs in her eyelashes. It was strange. She never had any form of gray hair before and now every time she looked in the mirror Valerie found herself staring back at silver lashes. She had to live with the hoary glance that made mascara her best friend. She was suddenly aging faster than she was comfortable.

Valerie had to admit, she was a little surprised how lonely June's death left her feeling since she had a big family. Her feelings of isolation had more to do with her relationship with June than with her family. June wore so many hats in Valerie's life, which was a miracle in itself being that she was so busy and lived far away. June was Valerie's sister, best friend, minister, life coach and therapist to name a few. Valerie spoke to her almost every day and about everything.

June was the nonjudgmental person who she would confess to; the carefree person who Valerie could say anything to; the person who would always tell her the unadulterated truth. June was the motivational speaker who urged Valerie forth. June was the counselor who allowed her to talk about 9/11 when the world had stopped talking about it openly, unless an anniversary was near. She had been so many wonderful things to Valerie. That's probably one of the reasons why she ran directly to June in Georgia, after 9/11, the first chance she had.

Although June lived far away, her death left a gaping hole in Valerie's life. There were specific times of the day that Valerie would tune out the world and simply talk to June. Valerie had to learn to fill those vacancies when people got used to her going away. It was hard sometimes because it was obvious to others why she had space to fill.

June and Valerie were the closest siblings in age. That's one of the reasons they got along so well. June was the only one who acted like a sibling. The others were more like having one too many parents. Valerie had to grow up in order to like them and realize they were supposed to protect her, instead of help plan parties.

Chapter 8

WHILE God's grace was always with Valerie, she was not always aware of it. It showed up many times, but one of the ways she recognized the Lord's generosity was believe it or not, through laughter. As funny as this time was not, there were times of laughter.

The family would be sitting in the family room and someone would say something utterly ridiculous. It would be something so stupid that you couldn't help but laugh. Some would laugh out loud uncontrollably. Others would smirk and try to hold it inside. Valerie didn't know what other people thought about it, but she was thankful for the rare comedic breaks from this awful reality.

The weight of the whole situation was too much, and then the laughter would seep into the situation. It helped to keep the family sane. It also temporarily leveled the playing field because reality was slowly trying to destroy them.

Recollections of June alone kept them in stitches. They spoke of childhood, and June's love-hate relationships with Jan and Valerie's friends, as well as boyfriends. They told stories of going to clubs. June would create a scene when it was time leave. Back in the day, Jan and Valerie partied until dawn and then had breakfast.

They also talked about June's behavior. It would be like day and night. Sometimes she would be like your best friend and in an instant, someone not to mess with. A younger June was easily pissed off. If you made her mad a plate would fly through the air. It's phenomenal how you can remember so many odd things about a person when you might lose them.

Another time the grace of God showed up was when Melody and Valerie were walking throughout the hospital. They were off on a self-proclaimed mission when Valerie found herself thinking about Samantha.

Valerie said, "Gees, I'm walking with the wrong sister."

"What are you talking about?" Melody questioned.

Valerie said, "You heard me. You know? If Sam were here, she would have found me a husband by now."

"I know, right? I thought about that earlier. Well, I guess you'll just have to be single a little longer."

There were many attractive men in and about the hospital. There were doctors, nurses, social workers and policemen everywhere. Under any normal circumstance, it would have been a single woman's heaven, but this was no paradise. It was quite the opposite.

The family had a long standing joke about how Samantha was always dressed up and beautified when going to a hospital. They'd make jokes about how she would always scope out the doctors for her unmarried sisters.

Valerie's wry sense of humor would not let her leave Samantha alone. She called her repeatedly. It was often way too late, so Candy would be asleep. Being in a hospital on a 24 hour bed watch tends to throw all sense of time out of whack. Valerie kept reporting back to Samantha. The truth is she felt like Samantha was missing something.

Once Valerie called and said, "I'm feeling your absence, Sam. You're costing me a man."

Samantha said, "I was just wondering if you met anybody."

"Well, the answer is no and you're going to have to pay for that." Samantha laughed while Valerie continued, "You would've caught them all, Sam. There aren't any really dressed up women in the hospital. You'd reel them in and then toss them to your sisters."

"You know I would"

They laughed over and over again. God was being kind by allowing them the ability to find humorous material. It was necessary not to get caught up in the negativity that was somewhat unavoidable. On many unforeseen occasions laughter supplied an escape. There were times when they laughed so hard they cried. It was like an unofficial version of group therapy. Samantha and Valerie continued their witty conversations in a manner that only they could. Only once, after June died, did Valerie interrupt the flow.

She asked, "Has Peter talked to you about what's going on? Or do you need me to fill in the blanks?

"No, I'm fine. Besides, he's on his way back to New York. He's going to drive us all to Georgia. If I have any questions they can wait."

"Okay, but if you want me to I can."

There were blessings on both sides of the knowledge tree. It was good being by June's side, but it was also a blessing to have been in New York.

God's grace started to grant Valerie peace. Undoubtedly, June's road home was Valerie's worst path travelled, but she learned to accept it. God knows what He is doing even if she doesn't understand. Perhaps, this particular journey was best for June. Valerie also accepted the possibility that this voyage was somehow a special part of positioning for a superlative passage for those left behind.

Part Four

Saying Goodbye

Chapter 9

JUNE had three jobs, but only one came with a desk and it was located at her full-time bank gig. Valerie wanted to collect any personal effects June had at work. Valerie called ahead, of course, so they knew she was coming. Mr. Daniels was nice enough to pick Valerie up and drive her to the bank. They got lost. They were in the right area, but just couldn't find the correct location for some reason. Valerie called the office for directions and was told to stay put; someone would come and act as their guide to the bank. So the two of them sat on the side of the road and waited. Shortly after the call was made, Janice came to the rescue.

It was nice to see a familiar face. After leading them to the appropriate building, Janice walked over to the car.

She said, "Come with me Valerie. I'll take you upstairs."

Valerie got out of the car and said, "I'll be right back, Mr. Daniels."

"Alright" he said, "I'll be waiting."

When Janice and Valerie got off the elevator people stopped and were staring. They had been waiting for a family member. Valerie was embraced many times, as June's co-workers asked about the family. Clare Richardson emerged from the small crowd and greeted Valerie.

She said, "Hi Ms. Valerie. I'm Clare, the receptionist."

"Hello. It's nice to meet you."

"You too, but I wish it were under better circumstances."

Clare hugged Valerie and walked her to June's cubicle. She pointed to several areas that housed June's personal effects.

Clare said, "These are June's work things and here is where you will find most personal things. I'll give you a moment. Take all the time you need." then she stepped aside.

Valerie was left alone in June's work area. She took a deep breath and sat down in the chair. *June's chair.* Valerie looked around trying to visualize June busy at tasks. She touched as many things as she could, knowing June had touched them. Valerie picked up the telephone receiver and held it between her ear and shoulder, typed out June's full name on the keyboard and gripped the desk drawer handles.

She gathered June's things. It wasn't much, but they belonged to June and should be taken home. Valerie began to feel overwhelmed and Clare reappeared with perfect timing.

"Ms. Valerie, some of June's friends would like to take a picture with you. That is if you don't mind. Would that be okay?"

"Sure. I don't mind, but I do have someone waiting for me."

"Don't worry, we'll be quick."

It was endearing. *Valerie thought these pictures will mean something. June really affected these people's lives.* They in turn, were now impacting the family in a profound way. The southern hospitality didn't stop.

After the visit, Mr. Daniels took Valerie out for a brief meal with two associates.

Mr. Daniels introduced his friends, "This is Ms. Francis and Mr. Williams. I've mentioned June Peterson to you, well, this is her sister Valerie."

"Hello. It's nice to meet you both."

Ms. Francis said, "I'm so sorry for your loss."

"Yes, we both are." Mr. Williams quickly added.

Mr. Daniels repeated, "Yes, we are.

"Thank you all." Valerie responded. "Now let us eat and try to relax a little."

During dinner, Valerie noticed Ms. Francis had beautiful hair and asked, "Can you recommend a good hair dresser?"

She responded, "Yes, of course. I'll get the information to you."

Valerie's hair needed to be done. She suddenly became extremely aware that she had been walking around looking like a hot mess. That was a first for Valerie. She had always been religious about getting her salon appointments. They were every two weeks on Saturday at 2 o'clock. She hadn't fixed her own hair since her early teen years.

Valerie returned to June's house where she decided to stay with the rest of the family. She washed her hair and tried to style it. It was a great thought, but it sucked in reality. She wanted to look decent, but her hair wasn't cooperating. She simply grabbed a light gray scrunchie off of June's vanity in the master bedroom. Valerie felt like a failure as she reached for it, but it was a fast solution. It also turned out to be a good thing for her life. Once Valerie put it on her head it stayed.

June's scrunchie provided Valerie with great solace during mourning. Valerie learned to reach for this generally insignificant hair accessory every time she missed her sister. At times it made her feel closer to June knowing she had worn it. Valerie loved being able to touch something that touched June, no matter how small. Who ever thought a ratty old now unscrunchable scrunchie would become one of Valerie's most prized possessions, but it did.

That evening after dinner, the entire Peterson clan was offered hair appointments, however, they didn't accept this gracious gift. They were extremely grateful for the heartfelt gifts being extended and there were many. The family only had time for these things in theory. The Petersons were preoccupied.

Chuck was becoming an issue. His attitude became increasingly bad and very noticeable. He wore the pain on his face. He missed his mother. Chuck was breaking their hearts further.

The family was desperately seeking a way to help Chuck to grow past the hurt. They wanted him to know everything didn't have to be awful going forward. They had each other. When you were there at the start of someone's life and have watched them grow up, you feel connected to them. That is the relationship that all of the adults had with Chuck.

It was a Monday when June started having labor pangs. Valerie was a teenager, but she stayed up with June all night. They did light exercises and tried to walk off the pain, but nothing helped. June and Valerie spent the better part of the night talking and timing contractions. It was a long and hard night. Valerie was happy to be by June's side, that is, until the adults forced her to stay home while they took June to the hospital. And then there was Chuck.

Everyone pitched in as a family should, and watched a handsome little boy develop. Fostering a relationship like that from the start makes everything extremely personal. Whenever Chuck was hurt, everybody felt impaired. Now that was happening on a large scale.

The real work was just beginning. There were arrangements to be made: family and friends to tend to, a casket, flowers and clothes to be selected for June, as well as a eulogy to be written. The family already had written most of June's tribute long before Valerie got near it. She simply had to add in her thoughts and edit the document. They had done a great job. June was amazing and all they had to do is put it on paper.

Melody and Valerie went to meet Melody's four friends and their cousin Diamond in front of the local supermarket. Diamond was a member of the PJS Girls, a singing group June, Jan, Valerie, Diamond and her sister Emma formed when they were young. The groups name was based on the cousin's last names. The P was for Valerie and June Peterson, the J was for Diamond and Emma Jameson and the S was for Jan Simpson.

People from all over the country were showing their love. Some gave assistance or flew into town. There were calls, emails and cards filtering into June's mailbox. There were countless family and friends in from all over the country. It was like pure goodness in the midst of a storm. Love and respect were being shown and it was appreciated. A decision was made to have June's wake and funeral in Georgia, due to the tremendous outpouring of love received. Her body, on the other hand would be laid to rest, in the tri-state-area.

Later, that evening dad arrived along with Samantha, Candy and Jan's daughter. Valerie has always been a complete daddy's girl. She was always ecstatic when dad arrived somewhere. This time was dreadfully different. His presence made everything real. For the first time in her life Valerie wasn't happy to see him. Dad, the original Chuck Peterson was no longer a traveler, unlike his younger counterpart who had seen much of the world. His elder self liked to stay close to home and had no intention of ever visiting Georgia. There was no insult, that was just the way it is and, the family knew it. In fact, dad frequently said, "No man my age that has seen what I have wants to go to Georgia." He never visited when the rest of the family did. Dad saw June and Chuck when they visited New York, which was quite often.

When dad surfaced at June's front door, it meant she had to be gone. His stature in the doorway confirmed it was truly final and June was dead. The fat lady had sung. This established that Valerie wasn't experiencing a nightmare and there was no waking up from this. Valerie's new reality strengthened with every step dad took. June's death bought dad to Georgia and Valerie hated it.

The first time Valerie laid her eyes on June's house was over the internet. It looked nice, but the picture didn't do it justice. Seeing it in person was magnificent. Valerie really liked it and was impressed with the internal architecture. They were all so happy for June. Valerie looked at every nook and cranny of the house. *She instantly thought dad's got to see this home.* His children have had houses, but not like this one. As a parent, it would have given him an extra sense of pride and accomplishment. Maybe it still did, but now it was the house that his daughter would never occupy again.

As Valerie rushed to pack for Atlanta that infamous Saturday, she was out of her mind. While she was overly aware of what was going on, all any of them could think of was June. Valerie never once thought about what footwear to put on because the pick would be whatever was closest. That was true for mom and Peter's packing theme, as well. They never planned to attend a funeral and their wardrobes didn't rise to the occasion. Valerie didn't have any shoes to wear and she also needed a suit—They were off to the mall.

Valerie travelled with family and friends. The suit she found quick and with no problems. The shoes, however, didn't work out as easily. Valerie couldn't find a pair of decent shoes. She had a mental picture of what was needed and never came close to finding it. They decided to look for a backup. Valerie tried to settle, but found nothing. The trip to the mall was quickly turning bad. Her mind kept wandering. *We still have so much to be done.* Valerie gave up; the problem was no one else had. She decided to go back to the house and that almost incited a riot.

Someone said, "Just pick something and buy it."

"It doesn't have to be the shoe you pictured, pick anything, it doesn't matter" another said.

"People will be watching," another agitated tone proclaimed.

"You have to be respectful. What will people think?" said another.

What will people think? Those words shifted Valerie's thoughts. Suddenly, she pictured a room full of people pointing and being horrified by her feet as she walked up to June's body. The image made Valerie angry.

Valerie yelled, "Anyone that cares more about my feet than the casket in the room can go to hell!" She continued, "I just don't care enough about the shoes. *She thought, June would understand.*

Valerie began to long for June. She was lost in a selfish abyss of loneliness. Their relationship was a close one. June was the sibling that Valerie spoke to the most. She was the one that was so quirky she made Valerie feel normal. The sister who made her want more out of life. She once told Valerie that she wanted to be more like her; going to school and getting degrees. Valerie wanted to be like June; widely independent and a go getter.

June was free spirited enough to go and find out where she belonged. She would search until the end of time for her heart's desire. June was beautiful and stronger than she ever realized. And now, she is the sibling that death has grabbed. The one they all lost.

Valerie felt like she was suffering. She had made it through so much that defeat was not acceptable. She couldn't display weakness now. Valerie announced, "I will wear what I have."

Diesels were not Valerie's first choice of footwear. They had a nice plain shoe look that served her purpose well. Better than that, Valerie's Diesels matched her suit and were very comfortable. That comfort was a Godsend because of all the recent physical and mental exhaustion Valerie had been experiencing. Her taxing physical ailments were not about to end anytime soon. Her shoes didn't matter. Their beloved sister was gone and she barely cared about much else at that point.

Standing there in the mall, Valerie wished everyone knew her better. They would have known that when she was uncertain there is a great deal of wiggle room on issues. And when her mind was made up there was absolutely none. She stood firm and confident in what it was that she knew. Regrettably, they didn't know her and time was wasted trying to change Valerie's mind.

After she unleashed the swift shout-fest, she was left alone. It wasn't the best way to handle the situation but she just couldn't take it anymore. Valerie hated being badgered. The last thing she shouted was, "I'm grown and my decision stands!"

Chapter 10

IT was time to go to June's wake. The family piled into a van and took a dire ride. It equated to getting in a car that's taking you to put your head in a guillotine. Just knowing where they were going was bad. Then they couldn't seem to find the place and that made it worse. The ride seemed like it would never end. Valerie wanted this day to be over and it was taking its sweet time beginning.

Eventually, they found their way. The family finally arrived and went inside. As the Petersons walked into the hallway, they saw family and friends. Diamond's sister, Emma threw her arms around mom.

Valerie had not yet made it fully inside like the rest of the family, in her attempt to do so she noticed a collage. The collection of pictures was located at the entrance of the aisle leading to June's body. It showcased June with various friends and family. It was a lovely distraction. Then Valerie turned left and looked down the aisle. There it was June's casket. It was somehow getting closer. Valerie was barely aware that she was moving toward it. *She thought the casket must be floating because surely I'm not approaching this thing that's cradling June's body.*

Valerie's children were sitting down in the front with mom and dad. They sat and watched their mother as she entered and Candy began to cry. Her tears shook Valerie out of her trance. She grabbed Candy's hand and walked outside into the lobby. Candy sat down on one of the couches and Valerie kneeled in front of her littlest baby. She was poised as if about to pray.

Valerie explained, "Wakes are different from funerals, baby. It's okay to walk in and out as we please. When it gets to be too much for you just let me know and we'll take a walk. Okay?"

Candy nodded and said, "Okay mommy." Then she announced, "I'm ready to go back in now." Candy was calm as she went back and sat down.

Angel on the other hand, sat silently bothered. She watched as others approached her aunt. Janice stood at the casket for a while. She was trembling and caused Angel to cry. Later, Valerie went to view June's body. She stood next to the casket for a long time. People came and went, while she stood in place. Prayers were whispered by some, while others were silent or crying.

Valerie knew that June would die one day. She had to subconsciously accept that one day far, far, away she might have to live without June for a few years maybe, but not now. June had always been there like all of Valerie's siblings; being the baby of the family. Valerie never really made way for the reality that June might not be with her in this world. And yet, here she stood over June's casket. Valerie kept staring down at June.

Part of her kept expecting to feel a hand on her shoulder and June's voice saying, "Why are you staring at that lady so hard?" Of course, that never happened. She just kept staring at June.

Valerie knew this might be the last time she would see June's body. She thought that she should take it all in. It was still so unbelievable. Standing there Valerie wanted to feel sick or angry, but the truth is she just felt numb. June's body was in front of her and she too was temporarily deadened.

Valerie glanced backwards and Diamond waved her over. So Valerie went and sat down next to her. Diamond handed her two brooches. The pins were small golden music notes that had a cross in the middle.

They were beautiful and befitting the close relationship they had growing up together.

Valerie said, "What's this for?"

Diamond replied, "I bought them for all the PJS Girls. One of those pins is for June."

"That's sweet."

"I figured you were the only one that would pin it on June, but you don't have to."

"It's alright, I'll do it."

It was that bitter sweet sentiment that led Valerie back to June. She headed back to the casket and lifted the veil draping over it. Valerie didn't intend on it, but immediately grabbed June's hand. It was puffy, stiff and cold. It had an unnatural feel, unlike the last time she held it.

In the hospital, June's body was being heated by some medical contraption intended to keep her body warm in case of organ donation. The chill on her body was startling. Valerie simply placed the pin inside her palm then returned to Diamond.

"I'm sorry, Diamond. I placed it in her hand without thinking."

"It's okay. You did better than I would have, thanks."

"You're welcome."

There was a visible sadness among the crowd, although, everyone appeared to be doing well under the circumstance. That is until Adriana, Jan's four year old, started asking questions.

Adriana asked, "Is that Aunt June, Mommy? Why is she in that box? Is she sleeping, mommy? Is she dead? Mommy?"

Jan shook her head no repeatedly and broke down in tears. She never answered Adriana's questions.

Valerie took Adriana to the side and answered, "Yes, that is Aunt June's body in the box."

"Why?"

"Because Aunt June went to heaven to be with God."

Adriana said, "It's great to be with God, auntie. I want to go to God too."

"It is nice to go to God when He calls you. To go before that is disrespectful and shows that you do not appreciate the great gift of life that He gave you. Do you understand, Adriana?" Valerie was confident in what she was saying.

"I think so Aunt Valerie."

"Well, if you have any more questions let me know."

Adriana said, "Okay." and never mentioned it again.

Adriana was satisfied and that was important.

Valerie remembered her grandfather's funeral when she was four years old. At the time, all Valerie wanted to know was why is grandpa sleeping in a box? And when was he waking up? Eventually, she wanted to know why he stopped visiting and why she couldn't go to heaven and see him. It's that simple for kids and adults sometimes complicate it.

Theresa was happy to see family from near and far attend, although she only found comfort during the wake from her cigarettes. She was often missing in action due to the increased volume of smoking she adopted in the hospital. In between puffs, she would greet family and friends.

Everyone had such lovely things to say during the wake, all except for Valerie. June's friends told warm stories. Cousin Edward told tales of birthday parties they shared. Diamond and Emma expressed their love at the podium as a team. A young lady that worked with June on the weekends read a poem.

Samantha said great things too and made a funny comment about June being the gypsy of the family who finally found a home. Samantha was great that way. She always had the ability to step up and do what the rest of us could not.

Valerie wanted desperately to get up and say something for June, but words failed her. There was no terminology that accurately identified the depth of emotion she was feeling. No thought seemed to say enough about anything. No one was pressuring her, but Valerie felt the need to speak. She was applying stress to herself internally. She sincerely doubted that anyone wanted to hear her speak, but she was a talker.

Valerie always had something to say. She was usually big on communication, but not today. Her thoughts were beyond the English language. There was no lingo that could summarize the enormity of her current mind-set. She would have fallen apart mid-statement. As much as she wanted to speak, she could not.

Thankfully, Valerie's words weren't necessary. There were endless family and friends who took the lead and shared their kind words and loved-filled stories. Who knows why someone chooses to stand up and speak, but it's helpful during a family's time of need.

As everyone took their turn and spoke, Valerie began to envision herself stepping up to the podium and delivering a sermon. Not for June because she's alright now, but for the rest of them who were not necessarily doing okay. Valerie's eloquent cerebral oration was about the Ways of the World versus the Ways of the Lord.

Ways of the World vs. the Ways of the Lord

On Saturday, April 22, 2006, the ways of the world viciously impacted my dear sister, June's life, as well as all of ours. June was in a brutal car accident that would forever change things as we know it. These past days have proven to be some of the toughest we have ever experienced and a race against time, possessing major struggles. We are hurt, angry, prayerful, and questioning anything that can be questioned of ourselves and the Lord.

On Wednesday, April 26, 2006, we received an answer. It may not have been the response we were looking for, but our question was answered nonetheless. The ways of the Lord lifted June up that day and made her whole again. I believe that our Father breathed a new and wonderful life into her soul. The ways of the world say stay down, be depressed and stay that way, but the ways of the Lord are to be happy and celebrate June's life and all that it meant to each of us.

The ways of the world say be angry and negative, especially when there is an easily visible target. The ways of the Lord say remain positive and screams forgiveness. The ways of the world focus destructively on how June died. The ways of Jesus say reflect on her demise as much you can bear and become better than you are.

Turn away from the darkness that calls while you are weak because the devil is a clever liar. Try your best to move past the pain. Use your pain so that someone else might experience beauty and rejoice in the love of Christ. Worry no more because June is well and God is good! Amen.

After the oration, the crowd erupted into applause. And someone handed out a lovely prayer card, as Valerie stepped down and was seated. It read:

> Do not stand by my grave and ask
> Are you cold? Or do you feel alone?
> I'm warmer than I've ever been.
>
> How alone could I be?
> Jesus resides in this new place with me.
>
> Do not wonder if I'm comfortable living in this box.
> The casket may contain my body
> But my soul is roaming free.
>
> Do not use my death to become angry or mad.
> Honor our relationship through Christ and be glad.

As soon as the vision ended, Valerie decided although she still had no words, she would go up anyway. She accepted the possibility of standing there alone saying nothing and washing her face with tears. Just as she found the courage, the funeral director approached the podium and announced, "This segment of the wake is now over."

Chuck said nothing either. He was simply sitting in the front pew, showing no emotion. There was no distressed look, no frown or anything. Chuck appeared as if he wasn't really present, while people cried around him. Everyone grieves differently, but he and Rick choose to handle it in silence.

Later that night, Valerie couldn't sleep. She got out of bed, left the room and went downstairs. Valerie could hear music and singing as she descended the steps. It was Theresa in the middle of the living room floor. She was singing into a hairbrush and dancing along with a Tyler Perry play. Diamond was on an air mattress next to her, which in this case meant front row center. It was hilarious.

One minute Diamond's face was filled with joy. The next, it had a panicked look that revealed a question. *Diamond thought should I get help? Has she lost it?*

The truth is that Theresa had found peace for a brief moment in the middle of this storm. Theresa was always good at finding her own joy.

This scene made Valerie happy. It reminded her of how they would do sing-a-longs as children and Theresa was often the ring leader. Valerie was thankful to Theresa for that skit she stumbled upon.

After the show, she went back upstairs and fell asleep strangely pleased. Valerie remembered Theresa gliding over the floor and laughing hysterically. Valerie forgot why she went downstairs, but she definitely got what she needed.

Chapter 11

THE limousines pulled up to the front of the house and awaited the family in the court outside of June's house. The funeral director's wife, approached Valerie and asked, "Who will be riding inside the limousines?"

Valerie couldn't think, so she listed names of people walking by them at the table. Thankfully they were the right people. Valerie's mind was focused on what they were preparing to go do. They were going to June's funeral and it was time to get into the cars and be on their way.

The ride was long and quiet. Once again, they were all going some place they didn't want to go; doing something they didn't want to do. Valerie sat in the last row of the limousine on the right hand side and continuously looked out the window. Many years earlier when they visited the South, cars would pull off the road when they saw a funeral convoy. In 2006, they kept driving and many attempted to cut across the procession. It was rude and inexcusable, but not a problem. The police escort that travelled with the Petersons on motorcycle handled these unfeeling road nuts in a swift and efficient manner.

Valerie stared out the window picturing June gliding alongside the vehicle. She was wearing an all white dress. June was smiling; her hair was luxurious and much longer than usual. It was four times longer than its normal length and blowing in the wind. June kept steady playful eye contact. This mental picture made Valerie feel like June was alright. Valerie always conjured up pleasant visuals after the loss of someone near and dear. Valerie no longer worried about them after their sightings and now, it was June's turn.

Once the family arrived at the church, they went inside. June's casket was open near the doors on the right. One-by-one they approached it and looked upon her body one last time. The Petersons sat down, not far from it. The family was relocated toward the pews near the altar. June's casket was now closed and followed them down the aisle and remained in the middle.

Much of the funeral was a blur for Valerie until she heard the voice of Father Mason. The family loved that Fr. Mason conducted the ceremony. His words were truly kind. Father Mason not only mentioned things typical of a funeral, he talked about the beautiful experience they shared during June's Last Rites in the hospital. Father Mason also read the eulogy and ministered to the people.

When the funeral was over, they walked down the aisle toward the doors. Samantha and Peter were hugging on the way outside; leaning on each other. They attended many funerals together but, this was different. This was the first time that Peter required assistance walking out of the church. In fact, Peter was usually one of those men who were overly helpful at funerals. Normally, he would immediately jump up at the conclusion of a funeral mass and insist on helping. Peter would tend to whatever was needed.

Very early on in life, Valerie became accustomed to seeing him carrying a casket, regardless of who it held. She kept waiting for Peter to spring to his feet, but it never happened. Instead, his steps appeared to become heavier with each one he took. He looked broken; they all did.

Father Mason was standing at the front of the church as the family exited. Samantha prayed that Peter didn't fall as she shifted his weight to shake father's hand. He had done so much for the family. He offered them a level of peace during an inconsolable time.

The family stood outside for a while as condolences were offered. Every kind word or hug that came their way felt like loving support. Most people came back to June's house and all were more than welcome.

Part Five

The Aftermath

Chapter 12

RETURNING home was bitter sweet. On one hand, it was great to be home and in a familiar space, but on the other, everything had changed, even in Brooklyn. The Peterson's lives had been drastically altered. They all seemed crazy or at the very least different.

Candy said, "It's like everyone forgot how to be themselves. It may be a natural response, but it doesn't feel that way."

Back in Georgia there was also a weird shift in the family atmosphere. June was gone and Chuck decided to move to New York. He knew that things would never return to normal. Everybody had been behaving strangely. They were themselves, but with a peculiar twist.

Every member of the family experienced a characteristic flip-flop. The happy go-lucky people were sad. The calm members of the family were riled up and shouting all the time. The non-dreamers were dreaming about what happened. And they all had to get used to mom blurting out June's name.

Watching mom scream was like watching pure concentrated emotion combust into the air. Like any explosion there were destructive particles left behind, which in this case were traces of unspoken agony. Immediately after yelling, mom's body language would declare that her mouth had betrayed her heart. The blast debris would hit those in her presence.

While in Georgia, Valerie had spoken with Angel's high school guidance counselor about her attendance; knowing she wouldn't be back for a couple of weeks. Samantha spoke to Candy's teacher. Once back in New York, Valerie had to write notes, and attach hospital and funeral letters. This was her way of making sure that both the girls were ready to return to school. She was trying to pay more attention to her children, but couldn't always connect the dots because she was lost.

Angel never complained. She appeared to be fine although she was not. She couldn't wait to get back to school. Angel needed a distraction. Her change was obvious, but Valerie couldn't see it.

Candy was ready to go back to school too. She thought it would be a nice escape. Her classmates knew why she left and showed sympathy upon Candy's return. It was a nice gesture, except, Candy took their concern for pity. Home was no longer normal and now neither was school.

Peter had always been hot tempered and controlling, but he got worse. There would be no respectful mourning period. He became violent towards Samantha ultimately wrecking their marriage.

Samantha's return was like no other. She had to deal with this new version of Peter and returning to work was no better. Instead of being greeted with patience and care, she found herself in the middle of more problems. Wherever Samantha went she could no longer sit still without bursting into tears.

Prior to Valerie's return to work, she decided to read, *The Purpose Driven Life* by Rick Warren. She loved how this book broke down the importance of 40 days in the Bible. It specified how wonderful things could occur during that time frame. *Valerie thought I need a phenomenal occurrence my life. I'll take this time to grieve and wear black for forty days while mourning for my sister.*

Valerie had always been the type of woman whose clothes reflected her mood. And her internal frame of mind was incredibly grim. She would read the book daily and wear black every day for 40 days. Valerie knew it would quietly say she was grieving and she was okay with that statement. This was how she allowed herself to mourn without fully accepting negativity. She was determined to be alright afterwards.

Taking this time was good because Valerie always responded well to deadlines. This daily tribute served her well. These days helped Valerie honor June while moving slowly forward. Valerie desperately needed something positive in place. She needed to feel better, even if it was only a little bit.

Valerie gathered all of her black pieces of clothing. She prepared outfits a week at a time. Valerie picked her clothes in advance because she didn't want any problems that might force her into another color. She wanted to wake up each morning and get dressed with ease. She bought one or two things to complete an ensemble, but that was it. Valerie was ready to go back to work with her mapped out clothing and letter in hand for her employer.

She didn't think her co-workers would care about her clothes. She figured it would be easily over looked. Once at work, no one mentioned she was wearing all black. The first day Valerie wore a splash of color the response was over whelming. Lifting the color embargo was to be a sign of hope. Walking in the hallways people complimented Valerie.

"Looking good one!" a person shouted as they passed.

Valerie yelled back, "Thanks!"

"Thank God, you're feeling better, Val, all that black was bringing me down." Someone said while getting on an elevator.

Even Valerie's boss, Mr. Megs, stated before a meeting, "Ahh, finally a hint of color."

"Yes sir."

"I hope this means that happy days are here again."

The display of color also affected her colleague's attitudes. Their expressions were brighter. Everyone smiled at her in the hallways. The people around her seemed to be filled with more cheer and that made her feel better too. Slowly, Valerie's clothes continued to get brighter. Something wonderful had taken place. Sadly, it was insignificant in comparison to her state of mind.

Valerie returned to work approximately two weeks after June's accident. Most people treated her normally, or tried, and then there was Ms. Stevenson. She stood out from the rest of her co-workers. The moment Ms. Stevenson saw Valerie, she embraced her. It wasn't any kind of hug. It was a deep, warm and lingering hold.

Valerie found Ms. Stevenson's affection rejuvenating. Ms. Stevenson would stop whatever she was doing, regardless of the importance and extend her arms when she saw Valerie. It seemed to be a basic instinct of hers that surfaced and it was a good one. For a moment in time, Valerie would not feel so alone. Valerie could breathe again, and not speak or answer questions. She was left alone in Ms. Stevenson's arms to be well.

Ms. Stevenson was like an intense five minute yoga class. They always seemed to cross paths when Valerie needed a little push. She didn't know why Ms. Stevenson felt this was a necessary action, but she accepted it. Valerie would encounter Ms. Stevenson all over the building: in the elevators, offices and conference rooms. *Valerie always left her thinking I can make it a little longer.*

At a later date, Ms. Stevenson shared with Valerie a personal story with great similarity in her own life. Ms. Stevenson knew things that Valerie could not have begun to know or process. For that reason perhaps, she knew Valerie needed unspoken support. A simple hug made an enormous difference.

Valerie decided to go through the motions, but she no longer felt like she fit in this life. She was trying to find her way back to normalcy whatever that meant, but was drifting through the days. At this point there was nothing she considered regular without June.

She was living in a disrespectful manner that didn't really consist of living. God had given her this life, but she wasn't really acknowledging it anymore. She merely existed. Valerie would get up and go to work just because June would if she could. June's tenacity helped her function.

Blessings come in all forms and from people that you would never expect. People would bond with Valerie through their personal tragedies. Many of which were so terrible they made her story sound like a joke. There were so many stories.

Valerie began to form a theory about all the chaos in the world. Many walk around with unexamined grief while the rest of the world unwittingly deals with it. Many loved ones left behind are walking around trying to put the pieces back together. Some mourners are successful while others continue to be angry with God and the world. These people often lash out at those around them making everything more difficult. It's so hard to contain these feelings, especially when they seem to fly in from nowhere.

Co-workers would share with Valerie that her presence made them feel strong. Valerie's boss, Mr. Megs had a story to tell. He informed Valerie that she supplied him with much needed strength a few times. Just knowing she was at work dealing with her situation with dignity helped him to not complain.

Valerie was called to a conference room for a brief party of appreciation for a staff member. Various personnel were gathered. Many were happy to be involved and others were biding their time. Valerie was silently beginning to have an anxiety attack. Valerie left quickly. It was only after she returned to her cubicle that she realized what was happening. Standing there, Valerie felt as if she were back in June's house after the funeral. It was a very similar situation. There was food, drinks and people just standing around somewhat awkwardly.

Outside of that instance, the only other time Valerie became that uncomfortable at work was at a company luncheon. It was the first gathering of its kind that she attended since being back from Georgia. Valerie was enjoying it until someone stood up and sang, *His Eye Is on the Sparrow*. Her face immediately tensed up as her eyes filled with tears. The song jogged a memory of singing to June.

Mr. Megs said, "Are you okay?"

Valerie didn't answer. She simply got up and ran out the room.

After that, Valerie involuntarily began to speak only when necessary. She preferred to write down her thoughts rather than talk about them. It had become too painful to share.

One day during lunch, Valerie went into the lunch room. There was a weekly ministry gathering happening in the middle of the lunch room. It was a group that offered appeal from the outside looking inward. Valerie expected nothing, but received everything. She didn't know exactly why, but this was one of the few places that Valerie felt good, so she kept returning.

It was nice hearing people discuss their own trials and tribulations and addressing them in the word. That was no easy feat depending on what was brought to the table. Nonetheless, Ms. Jenson, the ministry leader always worked wonders in her responses. She was careful to never push anyone.

Ms. Jenson would always ask Valerie, "Are you ready to talk?"

Valerie always said, "No, not this time."

"Alright, maybe next week."

Several weeks in, Ms. Jenson asked again and Valerie handed her a poem entitled, *Pain*. Valerie found it in a good book she was reading named *Black Love: A Book of Poetry & Love* by Alice Benton. Valerie had been carrying the book around because this poem represented exactly how she had been feeling.

Valerie first read this poem on Christmas Eve, traditionally one of the happiest days of the year, in her family. Every year was generally the same. The entire family would gather for an intimate Christmas Eve party. There would be an over abundance of food, drinks, music and love. Mom made great dishes while everyone else would sneak in what they called specialty drinks.

Jan would pull out her musical library of every Christmas song known to man. When the evening started the songs were great, but after a while it was too much. Depending on how loud the music protest got, mom would suggest a sing along. Everybody would chime in and bellow a note. The family loved singing holiday tunes. At twelve o'clock prayer was said in thanks for baby Jesus. Then gifts were opened. It was fantastic. Only this year was dissimilar. There was no party or singing, just silence, and memories of June while Valerie, came across the poem *Pain* reading *Black Love*.

When Ms. Jenson asked, "Are you ready to talk?"

Valerie pulled *Black Love* out of her purse, turned to page thirty-two and said, "No, but this poem is exactly how I feel."

Ms. Jenson gave it a once over then read it aloud to the group, as Valerie looked down and cried:

<u>Pain</u>

I thought I knew pain
On many levels
I've felt, seen and distributed my share
I've experienced extreme highs
Devastatingly extreme lows
But this . . .
This is some out of this world type hurt
I mean . . .
I truly never knew I could be so hurt . . . this hurt
I am completely and utterly devastated
I'm so bad that every inch of my body feels it
It's weighing me down
So I struggle
This pain is so deep
I don't even have to acknowledge it
Only to wake and be forced to recognize the pain
It lives behind the extra puffy eyes due to a tearful sleep
I struggle
I have felt lost and alone
Simply watching my life

No longer living it
How disrespectful
I struggle
I'm struggling with an unreal weight
This weight is so intense and intimately internal
It's potentially destructive
Surely, this is no natural heaviness
It's misguided wicked influence
The prince of darkness knows I'm divine
That's why he lurks in my madness
The devil likes when I'm weak, but I know he's a liar
Daily, I must convince myself of what feels inconceivable
Part of me is dead and worse
Evil is trying to use that lifeless part to kill the rest of me
I struggle
God just wants me to lean on Him
I have to rely on what I have always known
God gives you what you need to survive
Even if I don't know what IT is
It's there, in me
It's my job to struggle through
And so I struggle
Eventually, I'll win because God is good
I'm going to use this unique pain
Its distinct signature will elevate me toward an unforeseen destiny

After, Ms. Jenson read the poem the group encircled Valerie. They laid hands on her and prayed. Inside of that circle of love she found her voice again, albeit, slowly. It was a freeing experience. The ministry members like so many others carried Valerie through her worst days.

Some friends offered prayer, while others gave time. Many people occupied this grief-filled season wanting nothing more than to help.

Others attempted to use Valerie in her new found weakened state; instead they were used by God.

Valerie was finding it hard to concentrate. Her mind would wander and almost everyone would remind her of June in some way. She was on the beach with a friend and caught a glimpse of a small woman. Her frame and style resembled June's. Time stopped briefly as Valerie no longer paid attention to the conversation she was conducting. She was mesmerized as she watched this woman walk away.

Work wasn't always good. There were negative people wishing she would just get over it. One day, Valerie went into the lunch room, when Christina, a customer service representative and resident hater spoke loudly about her feelings.

Christina said, "I hate when people like you" as she pointed at Valerie, "use life to be so hypocritical."

"Excuse me."

"You heard me. It's like you'll do anything for attention."

"What are you talking about? I hear noise, but no facts."

"You want facts? Here's one, suddenly you've been wearing a cross every day. You have religion now because your sister died? No!"

Mind you, Valerie had been wearing that particular cross every day, since September 2004. A fact Valerie remembered easily because it was a graduation gift from June.

Valerie said, "I don't appreciate how insensitive you're being, Christina. You're showing who you are though because the devil is in the details. Why is it that you're only choosing to notice my "sudden holiness" because my sister died? Look, I have always had my faith. I was reared on it and am a believer. Thankfully, my mother taught me enough to know where to lean and how to survive. The only difference is I need it more than ever. When someone extremely close to you dies, you can easily lose the will to do the smallest things."

"Amens" bellowed around the room from lunch goers.

Valerie continues, "You don't want to get out of bed and if you do, washing may not seem important. I have been displaying my faith more, but not by wearing a necklace. I need it more and not for people like you who need something to talk about."

Truthfully, it took Valerie some time before she could really keep up with her usual routine. When she finally got back into the swing of things, she found new rituals and changed what no longer worked.

Another thing was happening too. Valerie kept running into people who had lost an immediate family member, before she lost June. She began taking on the weight of all those deaths. Valerie realized now that she just didn't get it.

She would see these people and feel like she should've done more; said more. Now, Valerie could recognize in them a sadness that she saw in her own face. She began to take more time not only with them, but with others who joined this awful club.

Chapter 13

VALERIE began to wander out of bed at night. Her mind suddenly became over active. Her thoughts would not subside long enough to allow some sleep. When she finally fell asleep it wasn't good. Valerie found herself wishing she were awake in order to escape the extra mental anguish she began to go through in the evenings. Her sweet dreams of June escalated into nightmares of overly graphic car accidents.

Valerie would witness worse case scenarios while asleep and associate them with June. She started asking herself questions like, "Is that the type of horror June went through?" or "Did she suffer like that?" Valerie's head would hurt instantly leaving her in a migraine-like state; waking up with headaches for the first time in her life. The pain was unbelievable. Valerie was being tortured internally, which led her to a phase of not sleeping. She did everything in her power to stay awake.

At first, Valerie simply wandered out of her room and down the stairs. She would sit up at the dining room table all night, not allowing herself to lie down. She hoped to become uncomfortable and unable to sleep, but that didn't work. Eventually, Valerie was so exhausted that she fell asleep virtually anywhere. It freaked the family out when they would find her in the mornings sleeping in a chair.

Valerie tried talking to the family, but they seemed to be down themselves. She didn't want to add to their depression. Valerie felt like she was disturbing them instead of getting some much needed help. Thus, she left them alone. When they were upset about June, which was most of the time, Valerie chose not to bother them.

She started calling her night owl friends to chitchat. Valerie wouldn't invite them into her misery, but they could hear it. One friend called Valerie on her melancholy mood and she never bothered her again. She was trying to escape her frame of mind and not have it analyzed.

The next solution involved taking to the streets. Valerie wandered around aimlessly in the middle of the night. The few times that people were aware of her behavior she received harsh judgment, but didn't care. Right or wrong, Valerie didn't feel it was anyone's place to judge.

Valerie tried to walk it out, hoping to exhaust herself beyond any form of unconscious thinking, but couldn't. Walking around was good for not falling asleep, but it wasn't good for Valerie. She was never into roaming around the city much. And as soon as Valerie came inside she would go to sleep. Good nights consisted of coming in and being surprised it was time to get dressed for work.

Sometimes Valerie would visit friends with the intent of talking the issue out of her system. One of two things would happen. She would either feel uncomfortable bringing June up and pretend it was a regular visit, or she would fall asleep. Valerie would rest for minutes only to be awakened by her own screams and people staring.

She struggled to remember the last time she felt comfort. Suddenly, Valerie knew what she had to do, call Lem. Lem not only had a great phone voice, he was a good listener. He covered vast territory while holding Valerie mentally and spiritually where she needed to be.

His tone made her think he was sexy as hell, but Lem meant more than that. He had a piece of her heart. Lem prayed with and for Valerie at times when she couldn't pray for herself. He would talk about things in relation to the Bible. Valerie would look them up to be on point knowing he'd mention it again.

Valerie had always been a praying person, but that ceased. It had become practically nonexistent; except where Lem was involved.

Keeping him was like holding on to her faith for a time. Admittedly, Valerie didn't want to pray, but her spirit was slowly rejoining the flock without owning up to it. Lem kept her in the word. He may not have had anything else, but he tried his best to keep Valerie speaking to God.

During one of their previous late night conversations, they decided not to meet once Valerie came back to New York. She was in such a vulnerable place and a crutch was forming. They began feeling really close to each other always talking and exchanging deep emotions. Lem and Valerie were connecting through this tragedy in a most unusual way. She seemed to understand him like no one else and he calmed her spirit.

They were beginning to lean on each other too much, having never met. Lem wanted to be careful and not take advantage of her. They agreed to wait and see what happened next. They felt it was a good decision, but continued to talk. Speaking made Lem and Valerie want each other more, so they stopped.

They hadn't spoken to each other since Valerie got back from Georgia, but now, she felt different. Valerie convinced herself she needed Lem. She was suffering and touring the city all night was becoming dangerous. She would run into all types of people and bad situations late at night. Valerie wanted to talk to Lem more than anything. She considered him a good friend and he already knew her situation. Well, beside this new development.

Valerie knew he would sympathize and be able to help. Lem would stay on the phone with her if she needed. It was hard staying away from him. Lem got her address from Gail and sent Valerie the sweetest card during this nonspeaking period. It read:

Valerie,

I've been keeping busy, but my mind always wanders back to you. I miss you and I'm sorry that I was unable to call. You know why I didn't. I hope you're well and that under the circumstances everything is fine.

Please forgive me for not being there with you during your time of need. Believe me, I'm not being as supportive as I would like, but I'm trying to stick to what we agreed you needed.

Be good baby girl and remember that God loves you . . . Personally missing you & sending a mental hug your way.

Lem

Receiving Lem's card made Valerie melt and it was the excuse she needed to call. She was many things, but rude wasn't one of them. Valerie had to call him back to say thank you for the card. She violated her own rule for the sake of proper etiquette and called him. When Lem saw the telephone number register on his cell phone he rushed to answer it.

He shouted, "Hey, Ms. V! How are ya?"

If a voice could make Valerie blush, his did. She said, "Good now that I'm talking to you."

And it was true. Valerie was good just being on the opposite end of the telephone line with Lem. She loved his deep sexy voice and it made her feel better instantly.

"So, how have you been?" Valerie said in a nervous voice.

"I'm good now too. I was just thinking about you, last night. Damn, girl, I really miss talking to you. I really want you too." Lem paused and then said, "Uh, I meant I really want to see you. I don't want to move too fast, but you're constantly on my mind. I was hoping you'd call."

He knew she'd call. Lem was on her mind too, he and his manly tone. Valerie loved talking to him. Hearing Lem say he wanted to see her was like magic. She wanted to see him too. She needed to see him. Lost in all that he was saying, Valerie jokingly mentioned how nice the mental hug was that he referred to in his note.

Lem laughed and took it an uncomfortable step further.

Lem said, "Hmmm, I was just going over that hug in my mind. I was wondering what it would be like to hold you for real. It felt good. Your skin was real soft, and I could smell your hair's sweet scent. It made me want to kiss you. I know you taste good."

Valerie couldn't believe what she was hearing, but continued to listen.

Lem said, "Not talking to you has been tough for me. It also made my mind go on overdrive. I'm not gonna lie; I've got the hots for you, V. It's like you're doing something to me even though we've never met. I'm wondering if what I'm imagining will slip over into reality someday. I want it to and I'm willing to wait very patiently. I can tell you're worth it."

Suddenly, Valerie didn't even know what they were talking about. She said, "Lem."

"Please don't interrupt, Val. I have to get this off my chest. I promised I wouldn't call you, but now that you . . . well, I just have to tell you how I feel. You melt me. I'm almost afraid to meet you 'cause we're already a couple in my mind. I don't know." Lem sighed, "I guess we made the right decision because I want you, so bad, and I want you to want me too. Don't say anything now. I just had to say that. So now you know. It's out there. I'm gonna let you go now, but if you need me for anything at all or you feel the same, call me back."

Lem hung up the phone. It was abrupt and a little rude, but Valerie was relieved. That conversation was unlike any they've ever had and she wasn't expecting it. Valerie wanted to respond, but she didn't know what to say. She was feeling all of those things, but they had never met. She wasn't going that route again with a faceless man no matter how good he made her feel.

Valerie called Lem back a few days later. She never actually told him why she called. She wondered how she was going to address their last dialogue, but decided not to put it off anymore. She would just wing it.

Valerie felt like a teenager. She was replaying scenarios in her head, but none of them turned out to be any good. She also got her "grown woman" on by writing out bullet pointed comments on an index card. All of this over thinking proved to be irrelevant.

The tables had turned. Lem was having an extremely bad day for a change. He had a huge fight with his younger brother, Lamar. Lem took it so hard when they fought. They became orphans young and it was just the three of them; the two brothers and Gail. For years since they were little, they had been everything to each other, second to no one else. That's how they survived.

Valerie wanted to assist Lem the same way he helped her, but he clammed up and wouldn't talk. Lem rarely shared any emotions about Lamar. Valerie got a little leeway when it came to Gail because they were such good friends. Lem assumed she knew much of her business.

She said, "Let me come over and be there for you. I promise to be silent if you need or at least not ask questions."

"Are you sure, V?"

"Yeah"

"Alright" Lem agreed.

Valerie knew it was a bad idea, but it felt right. She was having another sleepless night and it was almost three o'clock in the morning, but it didn't matter. She had to go.

Lem buzzed Valerie into his building and said, "I'm on the fourth floor."

Slowly she climbed the four flights of stairs, she began to smell weed. She huffed, "Damn, I'm too old for this shit," Valerie complained steadily hiking upwards.

She told herself it wasn't Lem, but it was. When she reached his floor there was a gorgeous muscular guy with a dark complexion, about six foot three inches tall, and a short hair cut standing in the doorway. He was wearing baggy jeans and a white wife beater that made his tattoos visible. He was smiling widely.

"Valerie?" Lem asked.

She answered, "Yeah, it's me. Lem?"

The mere sight of this man standing before her made Valerie happy. She could finally add a face to the sexy deep voice over the telephone. Their pleasure at first sight was obvious.

"Yeah! Wow, you're sexy! Don't worry, I'll behave. Come here baby girl," he said with his arms now wide open and ready to embrace her body, "I can't believe you came, V."

The truth is she shouldn't have. Valerie was using all he had done for her as an excuse. Valerie was really happy to finally meet Lem face-to-face, but she didn't know this man. It was too late to worry about that now because she was standing right in front of him. Lem held her tight as they walked backwards into his apartment. She instantly felt a contact high from both the weed and his body. Valerie had never tried marijuana and the heavy stench in the air made her instantly loopy.

Every alarm inside of her body was going off and being ignored simultaneously. Valerie's intuition was telling her to run, but she refused to give into her inner track star.

Lem said, "Please tell me if I'm making you uncomfortable. I'm just so happy to see you. I've been waiting a long time for this."

Valerie was relieved to hear him say what she was thinking because she was all too comfy in Lem's grasp. Feeling at ease came natural with Lem. He'd been her man on a mental low for at least a month.

They talked a little bit, but they were at a loss for words. Habitually staring at one another as the other person looked elsewhere. Lem continued to hug Valerie as they sat on the couch and pretended to watch television. She leaned her head on his shoulder. Then out of nowhere, Valerie tasted a Lem flavored kiss.

"Hmm," he moaned, "finally, that was great."

Valerie's brain was screaming, yes it was, but she said nothing. She reacted stunned, like a young teen finding out what it means to French kiss.

He stopped and apologized whining, "I'm sorry, V. I've wanted to kiss you and couldn't take it anymore, but it won't happen again, not unless you want it to."

Excitedly Valerie proclaimed, "Don't worry about it" although she was nervous and breathing heavy. "Can I have a look around, a tour perhaps?"

Lem smirked looking her up and down and said, "Sure. You can have anything you want, but there ain't much to see." He jumped up and said, "This is the living and dining room. The bathroom is in that corner to your right. The kitchen is here to your left." Lem grabbed Valerie's hand and pulled her to her feet. They walked through an old fashion beaded curtain that led to his bedroom. He laughed and said, "And this is where the magic happens. Let me get the lights on for you."

As he reached for the string in the middle of the room she reached for him. This time Valerie kissed Lem. Their kiss was powerful this time. Valerie pressed everything that belonged to her against him forcefully as she attempted to hypnotize him with her tongue. She pulled away briefly, not to seem desperate, but she wanted him. Valerie wanted to touch him.

Lem was completely mesmerized by her advances. He waited patiently for her next move. Lem was now following Valerie's lead, but his eyes showed that he wanted to devour her body. Respectfully, he waited to see where she was going with this.

She rammed her tongue down his throat again. Valerie groped Lem a little and threw her right leg up and around his body. She felt like she'd gone too far. Valerie pushed him gently and left the bedroom quickly.

She yelled, "I've got to go!" and kept moving until she was out the door and down the steps. Valerie heard him calling her name, but she kept going.

Every time Valerie thought of Lem afterward her face exuded embarrassment. She needed him but was no longer sure about calling. Valerie was becoming worried. It had been a few days and he hadn't called her either. Valerie received a short and sweet email from Lem. It read:

> V,
>
> I'm sorry I haven't called, but I just didn't know if you wanted me to. You ran out so quick and never looked back. I figured I should give you some time to work it all out for yourself. I never want you to run from me.
>
> FYI, baby girl, I never imagined that just kissing you would be that good. Your soft lips rocked my world. It left me woozy thinking about what it would be like to be with you. I kept reliving it in my dreams each time going a little further. I may not deserve your love, but I sure want it.
>
> Let's be clear, I miss you and I enjoyed every moment we shared, but if it's too much, tell me. I won't like it, but I'll understand. Please talk to me, babe.
>
> Yours in any way that you need,
> Lem

Valerie had to call Lem because her mind interpreted that as being safe to go back into his world. Well, that's what she wanted to believe it meant. They spoke and decided that she would visit him, but it would be different this time. As Valerie climbed the stairs she smelled weed again and wondered how long she was going to ignore it.

Lem greeted her at the door with open arms and an innocent kiss. They walked inside hand-in-hand this time and he said, "I'm glad to see you. I didn't think you'd ever come back."

It was worse this time. It appeared their link had been severed. You could cut the tension in the air with a knife. There wasn't much being said and he was uncomfortable.

Valerie asked, "Did I make a mistake coming back?"

"Why do you say that?"

"We're not talking, you seem uncomfortable and I'm starting to feel like I shouldn't be here. Why are you acting like this?" He looked at Valerie, but continued to say nothing. She urged, "Tell me."

"I just want you to be alright while you're here. I don't want you to think I'm scheming on you. I don't want you to leave me again."

"This is your house. How am I supposed to be alright in it when you're not?"

"I'm acting this way because I keep thinking about the last time. So I'm keeping my distance. Okay?"

"So you're never gonna touch me again?" she said worried.

"Of course I will if you're sure you want me to, I'm just taking it slow on my part."

There was only one thing Valerie could do . . . she kissed Lem more passionately than last time demonstrating no self-control. For some reason, unbeknownst to her, she didn't have any. The kissing led to touching. The touching led to clothes being removed while they went into the bedroom.

Lem placed her on the bed and said, "Please tell me if you want me to stop. Don't run."

Valerie should have said something, but didn't. Part of her wanted to stop so that she wouldn't regret it, but there was another piece of her that was growing stronger. It was being satisfied. This behavior she was so willing to go with was out of character. Valerie never acted like this, until now.

The longer it went on the more alive Valerie felt. Feeling alive was good. She had inadvertently been over thinking her mortality. All of this naked bustling behavior was beyond amazing and nothing had even happened yet. Valerie knew she should stop, but had to continue. She wanted to find out how full of life she could become.

After sticking his tongue in it, Lem whispered in her ear, "I think I love you."

Valerie smiled, but said nothing.

He repeated it in between kisses on her neck, "No, I know I love you, Val. I love you."

She made a face.

He continued, "Come on, baby, just say it."

Valerie smiled again more awkward.

Lem stopped sharing his kisses. He took his hands off of Valerie's intimates and held her arms down firmly. He stared into her eyes and stated in a stronger tone, "I know you don't love me, V, but I want to hear it anyway. Please say it. I need to hear it, baby. Now . . ." there was a long pause before Lem repeated, "I love you." He waited patiently, staring into her eyes, as she breathed heavily pressed against him.

Valerie hesitantly said, "I . . . I love you too."

Once he got her to say it, she never stopped. From then on, every time Lem proclaimed his love, she did too. Valerie learned quickly that those words were a precious commodity to him. He needed to hear it and didn't seem to mind whether she meant it or not. It worked for them until Christmas the following year.

Valerie had spent the whole day with Lem. They had a fabulous time. Once inside, Valerie sat on the couch and was in heaven. For a change, she said it first, "I love you, baby."

At first, Lem gave her a long hard gaze and his eyebrows were scrunched together. He got up and poured Valerie a glass of red wine, then sat down. He had that look in his eyes. That let me ravish you gaze. His body language was supporting it too. Lem grabbed Valerie's feet and took off her sexy heels.

She smiled because his foot massages were off the hook. At the end of it Valerie was ready and giving off some body lingo of her own. Everything this man did was sexy. She couldn't resist. Valerie swung her feet down and attempted to push Lem on his back by leaning over on him.

He gently pushed her back up and said, "Val, do you love me?"

She quickly proclaimed, "Yes!" as she tried to push him once more, but was unsuccessful. "You heard me, I said, I lo . . ."

"Shhhh, just shush," he said, placing his index finger over her mouth. "Do you really love me? Please don't lie."

Valerie sighed and said, "You know I have love for you." She puckered up and leaned forward to be shoved in reverse this time.

"This is the last time, I'm gonna ask you and you better answer me right! Truthfully, are you in love with me, V? I need to know! I'm in love with you and I deserve to know if that love is being returned!"

Valerie got up off the couch and looked out the window.

He continued, "It didn't matter before, but it's all that matters now. Do you love me? I need to know what's up with us. Huh?"

Valerie said, "I" then paused.

Lem picked up her wine-filled glass took a sip and threw it. It shattered on the wall near the window where she was standing.

Valerie turned around completely shocked.

"Stop looking out the fucking window!" he screamed.

Valerie screamed, "Of course I'm in love with you!" *I don't mean it, but never piss crazy off, especially in unprecedented moments.* "Shit! Did you have to throw the glass?" Trying to lighten the moment she said, "What did it ever do to you?"

Lem questioned, "Then why did it take so long for you to answer me? I don't know if I can believe you now." Lem said walking over to Valerie. He kissed her lips and gave her a hug. "Damn, why couldn't you just answer?" He laughed wiping specks of wine from her face.

Valerie said weeping softly, "I just wanted to let you know it's real in my own time, not yours, but I guess that didn't matter. It'll never happen now. Are you happy now?"

"Hell yeah!"

"I do love you, but we fell into this too fast. And that glass shit reminded me that we don't really know each other."

Lem said, "We know all we need to know and I'm never letting you go, Val. Let's go into the bedroom and make love."

"Alright, give me a minute." Valerie was shaking. She went into the bedroom and said, "I don't really feel like it. You got me on edge. I think I'm gonna go home and get some rest. Let's connect tomorrow, okay?"

"No."

"What? No?"

"Nah, you told me you really love me for the first time. I want you and I want you now. So get over here and tell me, whose is it?"

Valerie thought when you have to ask you already know whose it isn't. She didn't answer.

Lem clutched Valerie's hair roughly in his hand to control the direction of her head while he kissed her neck. He pulled her down into the bed.

Valerie said, "Lem?"

He was smiling and said, "That's right. Now, the question and answer segment is over. Talking is no longer acceptable for the night, shhh." Lem Laughed and said, "Don't make me get another glass. I'm ignoring what you want to say on purpose."

Valerie's statement was no longer important. The message was received. It didn't matter anyway because Valerie was going to announce she was leaving, which she didn't. Somehow Valerie knew it would be better for her if she stayed.

This time Lem made it hurt. He leaned in on Valerie with his eyes closed in a way that felt unnatural. He stared and smiled while she was in pain.

Valerie said, "You're hurting me."

Lem shook his head and smirked. He was enjoying it. Lem watched as tears rolled down Valerie's face and kept going. He stared into her eyes and pressed harder until he was finished.

She hated it. This experience was vastly different from all their past encounters. If he shifted a little she might have enjoyed it, but he didn't care. She wasn't meant to enjoy that.

The time before this incident, Lem had questioned Valerie.

As they fooled around, Lem asked, "Will you let me take care of you? Lem smiled and said, "I'll take care of you if you let me, alright ma?"

Valerie nodded yes intensely then tried to kiss him, but he pulled away.

She screamed, "Boy, you better kiss my lips now!"

He laughed and said, "Okay."

Lem spread her legs, positioned his head between them and puckered up. He took care of her for hours. He wanted to make her happy. Lem was unlike anyone she had ever known. He felt like a best friend, even though he was just the best.

Hours later, Valerie was feeling pain. It had reached places long forgotten. Her whole body hurt, but it was worth it. She was exhausted and unable to think or sit straight.

There was no longer any reason to question being alive because she was feeling too good. The world seemed to have a whole new ambiance. Afterwards, Valerie certainly felt like she loved him and that's exactly how she got caught up. Her body did anyway. Valerie already knew she was going to wake up late, but tried to avoid it by setting the alarm on her cell phone.

The first time Valerie slept over, Lem's cell phone woke her up. It started ringing at around seven in the morning. He didn't budge, but she had a sinking suspicion that he was awake. Valerie was too tired to care, but she remembered falling back asleep again with that feeling in her stomach. *Her mind was screaming who the hell was that?* When she woke up again, they were late for work. They called in and laid there unable to function for a while talking, then she dosed off again.

Now, Valerie woke up confused and uncomfortable about the previous night they had. She recalled Lem hurting her and not letting her speak. She was really bothered by the whole situation, but they acted like there was nothing wrong.

Valerie had been depending on Lem hard and fully expected him to keep her whole. She was strangely tranquil in Lem's presence and slept calmly; there were no nightmares, only peace. Her sleep was deep and she loved it.

When Valerie finally woke up she was alone. She was feeling refreshed and surprised that she stayed so long. As Valerie walked through the apartment looking for Lem she noticed that he cooked. Two plates of food were placed on the table, but he was in the bathroom. She approached the door to comment on the food. She could hear the shower running and he was already talking. Valerie couldn't hear what he was saying.

She said, "Speak up honey."

He kept talking, but didn't talk louder. Lem came out of the bathroom with his cell phone in hand and kissed Valerie on the cheek. He gestured for her to sit down and eat. Lem had been talking on his phone in the bathroom, with the water on full blast.

That's a pet peeve of Valerie's; a serious no-no. There are one or two exceptions to the rule, but for the most part, that's a cheater's move. Valerie looked at Lem with disgust in her eyes while remembering a serial cheater ex-boyfriend. That foul blast from the past made her feel like she overstayed her welcome. *She then thought did the kids get to school?* It was time to reenter reality and be responsible.

Initially, Valerie knew she would be back, but now she wasn't so sure. She never should have been there in the first place. She wanted to call Gail, but didn't feel she could. They hadn't spoken much since she became involved with Lem. Valerie didn't think she would tell her anything about Lem anyway. Gail was tight lipped about her little brother.

Unfortunately, returning was inevitable due to Valerie's sleeplessness. She wanted to be in his life for the time being although they didn't really fit. She had a bad feeling about Lem, especially with all of the early and late calls he'd ignore. She could tell something was up with him, but permitted herself to overlook it to meet her own needs.

Valerie could see the symbols of chaos that were staring her in the face. Like the pink toothbrush that would appear and disappear that he said was his daughter's. The pictures she would stumble on that were supposedly old or the long hair she saw on the inside of the bath tub that didn't resemble her own. Valerie didn't want to see the signs. She wanted to love Lem, if for no other reason than timing.

Valerie convinced herself that she trusted Lem. She decided to call Gail, but only reached her voicemail. Gail was no longer available. She was beginning to believe that Gail was a fictional character she created.

Valerie was managing her mornings badly. She would always oversleep causing her to call home. Valerie would literally give her girls a wakeup call for school. Then she would speed off late for work.

She never managed to hear her alarm, but always heard his landline and cell phone ringing. She paid attention to his body language and could see when he was faking sleep. Valerie would take note if he would answer and listened to how he spoke when on the phone. The tone a man speaks in is telling.

Their relationship went on without a hitch until Lem and Valerie started talking about being a serious couple. She didn't want to have that conversation, but it wouldn't go away. Lem kept bringing it up. They were already so immersed in each other, but realistically they were worlds apart.

Lem continuously complained about not being in her children's lives, but it couldn't happen. He personified everything she'd told them to run away from in a man. Lem lived a gangster lifestyle. Any half-way decent parent wouldn't expose their children to Lem. His everyday life needed to change and Lem inferred daily that that wasn't happening. He would tend to all of Valerie's needs, but became increasingly distant.

The beginning of the end was becoming clear. It was reaffirmed when Valerie started receiving numerous hang-ups on her cell phone. Shortly after that episode began, Valerie received a telephone call from a woman named Neesa.

Valerie said, "Hello."

Neesa responded, "Hi, I'm Neesa, Lem's girlfriend."

"Did you say his girlfriend?"

"Yup! We've been together for almost four years. And who are you?"

"Wow, I've been Lem's girlfriend for over a year now."

Neesa screamed, "Stay away from my man, bitch! You mean nothing to him! He does this shit all the time and this is no different! So back off!"

Valerie responded, "You don't have to worry. I don't want him anymore and I don't know why you do either. You can have him all to yourself."

That was just the beginning, but the writing was finally on the wall. Too many questions would pop up, Neesa changed her tune. They swapped details leaving nothing unturned. They realized that they worked opposite schedules so they never clashed.

Lem on the other hand was a hustler. He was home when he felt like it, which made things really easy for him. He decided when to work and when to stay home and play. He was in complete control.

Valerie began being unavailable whenever Lem reached out in her direction. They would speak briefly, but Valerie would always be quick to get off the phone. She never let on about Neesa because she was trying to avoid drama. Valerie thought about mentioning it, but remembered the wine glass and said nothing.

Valerie missed him a little, but that was it. She had enough problems without having to worry about other women and diseases. She recently tested herself because of the various broken condoms and slip ups, but felt an immediate need to do it again.

At the doctor's office a new young student doctor made things easy. The student said with extra spunk in her voice, "Well, what brings you to the office today?"

Valerie was on a small medical table. *I should have followed my instincts.* She replied ashamed and in a low voice, "A new boyfriend slip-up."

The young doctor in training asked, "Would you like the new boyfriend slip-up total work-up with all the trimmings to be safe?"

"Yes, please. Test me for everything."

It was as simple as that. She didn't even have to ask for anything. Just like that it was over. Luckily, Valerie received a clean bill of health.

Neesa called again. She wanted to talk about a plan. Neesa wanted Valerie to do her a favor by backing her up and confronting Lem. Their affiliation was odd. It was like an old relationship that she couldn't get away from.

Valerie wanted to move past it. She hated talking to her, but did because she was victimized too. Valerie wanted to stay out of it, but didn't want to leave her in a bad position to spare a manipulating man. It took a little prodding, but they came to an agreement. Valerie refused to physically be a part of anything, but would be helpful.

Originally, Neesa wanted Valerie to be with them as things unfolded.

Neesa asked, "Will you come over to Lem's house?" Neesa wanted too much. "I'll be over there in approximately ten minutes."

"No. That's not happening."

That was more than Valerie was willing to do. As far as she was concerned, it was over. Valerie had already checked out of the Lem madness. She was sleeping better too. Valerie wasn't going back into the lion's den with a new territorial lioness on the prowl.

"I understand. Ok, new plan, Valerie. Wait about twenty minutes and call my cell phone. I should be with Lem."

Valerie was hesitant, but said, "Alright, twenty minutes."

As Neesa's cell phone rang, *Valerie thought what the heck am I doing? I should hang up.*

Neesa said, "Hello."

Valerie could hear Lem laughing in the background watching television. She noted the sound of happiness.

"Neesa, this is Valerie."

"Are you ready?" Neesa asked.

"As I'll ever be, I can't believe I even called so let's get it over with quickly."

Neesa said, "Alright, hold on."

Valerie heard Neesa saying, "Someone wants to talk to you."

Lem said, "Sure, babe."

He didn't even ask who it was. He must have talked to her people often. He never spoke to Valerie's, but she didn't want him to anyway.

"This is Lem." he said, still chuckling.

Life was good for this motherfucker. He had two women and Neesa was suspicious of more.

"This is Valerie. So you have another girlfriend, huh?" There was dead silence. Valerie thought he hung up.

He got it together and said, "Who is this?"

"You know who this is. Neesa told me you've been together for four years now. I'm so disappointed. I could've just used a friend, ya know?"

"No, Val, I'm disappointed in you. I can't believe this shit! I never thought you would betray me like this. I loved you."

"You have some nerve."

Then the line went dead for real. He hung up.

Neesa called back, but Valerie didn't answer because she had had enough of both of them. Neesa left a thank you on Valerie's voicemail and asked her to call her back, but they never spoke again. She was crying, on the message. Neesa claimed he would have never been caught if Valerie hadn't helped because the obvious lies sound like truth when in love. That communication was all Valerie needed to hear. She let him go for good.

Lem tried to reach Valerie quite a few times, but she avoided him like the plague. He left long messages that consisted of apologizes and tears. He claimed to have dumped Neesa but she didn't fall for that. It wouldn't have mattered anyway. Valerie shifted into a whole other space. He'd say, "I love you" and plead for her to let him explain. Then Lem graduated to screaming messages.

On one message, Lem let Valerie know he had made a mistake. He should have thrown the glass in her face. Another was filled with him shouting his disappointment. It was crazy for a while.

She learned to screen all her calls, but never developed any animosity toward him. It may not have been what she needed, but Lem helped Valerie through a rough patch in her life. Her thoughts about it existed in the realm of the Lord giveth and taketh away. In all actuality, she didn't think the Lord placed her in that bad circumstance, but he certainly found ways to use it for her good.

Valerie knew they weren't meant to be together, although she had successfully ignored many of the previous signs. A while back during her relationship with Lem, a lump was found in Valerie's breast. She of course followed up with a mammogram and ultrasound. Friends and family prayed with and for Valerie constantly. She also did her part; thanking God repeatedly for it already being taken care of by His stripes. Valerie prayed over the lump night and day with loved ones. She was thankful to have had so many people in her corner, except Lem. She wasn't his priority.

Lem stayed away during this ordeal. He was always going through something whenever Valerie needed him. When you love someone who's frightened and dealing with the possibility of cancer you don't disappear. Miraculously, the lump disappeared. This new development was disappointing, but they both knew that their tryst had run its course. It wasn't painless, but it supplied a quicker exit than she could. It was time to stop being distracted and get on with life.

Lem crying about their love was laughable. A man who loves you doesn't have an affair. He doesn't knowingly open you up to diseases. A man who loves you doesn't introduce you to bad things. Lem tried to peak her interest in many bad things. Valerie wasn't down for any of it. A man who loves you doesn't threaten or hurt you. Love was non-existent in their relationship.

Lem made Valerie feel good during a time when everything hurt. He showed her how to breathe when she was drowning. He picked her up when she could care less about ever standing again. Lem helped her during a period when she hadn't sufficiently learned how to save herself.

Valerie wanted to love Lem for those reasons, but didn't. It would have been hard to leave him without the Neesa bomb dropping, but that was the least of her worries. The timing of their union was perfect, but then so was its demise. The desire to love isn't the same as being in love. Later on, they tried to reconnect as friends, but couldn't. Life was literally getting in the way. It was for the best. Their season had ended.

Chapter 14

NEW Year's Eve, the family was invited to numerous events. There were small social gatherings, huge black tie galas and of course the option to attend church. The Petersons decided to stay at home and be together. They held a small family party and things felt alright. Valerie had her girls and most of the immediate family around. The music was great and the food was phenomenal. The atmosphere was daring them to feel good.

Finally, the New Year had come. *Valerie thought this is a new lease on life.* Hugs and kisses were shared around the room. She went into an immediate prayer of thanks to God.

Valerie prayed, "Thank you Father for bringing my whole family safely into this New Year . . ." Then Valerie became enraged and couldn't finish. Her whole family hadn't made it safely into the year. Valerie suddenly realized that she was furious with God.

God had allowed June to be taken. Why should she be happy about that? Spiritually, Valerie's beliefs would generally push her to rise above the fury, but not now. She needed a moment for this to pass and time was not on her side. She didn't want to be mad at God, but it was a fact. This problem was cheapening her life.

Eventually, Valerie acknowledged that even though she was separated from June, they were both still with God. Neither one of them was alone nor would they ever be. Had Valerie accepted this earlier, the misery would not have continued as long.

Valerie attempted to pray, but her efforts were disingenuous. She tried many times after the New Year, but could never continue. Valerie kept trying to pray. She knew it would be indisputable when it was authentic. She was prepared because her good friend, Elder Jim, warned her about being angry with God.

Elder Jim said, "It will take you by surprise, but there might be a time when you'll realize that you're mad at God."

Valerie said, "Never."

"I'm serious, Valerie, so please listen to me. If that happens, be very careful not to run with that feeling. It will be easy to let go in the middle of your pain and embrace bad feelings toward the Lord. You always have a choice. Don't run with it."

They spoke many times of things relating to death and grief. Elder Jim became Valerie's unofficial grief counselor and confidant. She had to learn not to be angry and Elder Jim helped her through those feelings.

Valerie knew she shouldn't be upset, but apparently her emotions were unaware of that fact. It helped knowing that what she was going through was normal. She never really deserted the Lord and more importantly, He never abandoned Valerie.

Chuck had become a new resident to New York this year, but often stayed to himself. He had a good head on his shoulders, but knew that he could very easily become overwhelmed. Never before had he dealt with household things. Chuck was a legal adult, but still very young and on his own for the first time.

One day while visiting, Valerie asked Chuck, "Are you happy mom pushed you to move to New York?"

"Well, I know why she did it and she was right. It's good to be around everyone, especially since Theresa and Rick moved back.

"Have you been praying?"

Life's irony was showing. The person who had previously found it difficult to pray was now pushing it.

Chuck replied, "No" accompanied with a crazy look.

"I recognize it might be hard right now, but keep trying. Believe me, things can change when given the chance. Do you still believe in God?"

"I'm not sure," he said with disappointment in his voice.

"That's disappointing, but I think you do. You just don't want to right now. Please don't give up on God, Chuck. Prayer will come later. I trust that you'll find the words when the time is right."

Valerie decided that she would believe enough for the both of them.

Chapter 15

THE grieving process meant a different thing to each family member. Their various personalities with each person's distinct traits shined during their grief. Every person took part in a uniquely personal mourning period. They never really spoke about what they were going through independently, which didn't allow them to relate to one another in grief. Some of them became more introverted while others became extroverted. The Petersons new selves were emerging. While these grief stricken emotions were brought on by the same event, the process separated them.

They did share some of the common traits of grief like numbness, yearning for June, unstable emotions, and bargaining. Valerie's numbness came and went, but it wouldn't stay for long. Being numb was a welcome feeling at times because when it was present she felt no pain.

In many attempts to try and cope with June's passing Valerie began to ask questions. There were too many to count, but, at least one lingered for a while. *"Why June?"* She'd verbalize to the Lord, "June was a good person and most people were not as sweet. Why did June die, Lord?" Valerie never got the omniscient answer she wanted, but she did find a response she thought acceptable. The Bible refers to the righteous perishing. In Valerie's life, she had found that to be true.

Valerie theorized once again. She had to hypothesize when a clear answer would evade her questions. That's just how she was. While relaxing with friends, Valerie would begin to speculate, holding them captive to her thoughts. Valerie came to believe that when negative things happened, and good people died, it was possibly because they didn't need more time to get things right.

Valerie was in the middle of a get-together when she blurted, "Good people are ready, for a heavenly debut!"

Her friends looked around the room at each other worried and feeling sorry.

Valerie persisted, "Yes, they have already learned life's lessons and were rewarded with eternal bliss. It's not a punishment. Those left behind, like us, are being given a second chance. I know I strive to be righteous. I even nail it sometimes, but things still need to drastically improve."

As for yearning, that's one characteristic that Valerie felt almost immediately. The longing for June was instantaneous. It too would come and go, but when the deep desire for June seeped into whatever was going on, it would pierce her heart. The strongest yearning episode was on the day June died. The next time it hit so deep was during a speech Valerie made at an event over a year later.

During the affair, Valerie started to comment on how the past year had been hard. She looked around the room. *June would have loved to see me in action speaking to my colleagues.* Valerie could barely speak. She cut her speech short, finishing all too quickly and began to cry. Valerie's stomach ached and her heart panged. She wanted June. She could barely focus although she was struggling to pay attention.

Mr. Megs was talking to Valerie as she sat in a corner not far from the podium tearing. She couldn't see who it was or hear what they were saying.

Mr. Megs said, "Valerie? Valerie? Can you continue?"

The answer was clearly no because Valerie sat there shaking. When she finally answered she spoke out of place saying, "I miss my sister."

Valerie's emotions were sporadic. She was going through bouts of sadness and tried to perfect her bargaining technique. She attempted to negotiate a good deal with God during June's last days. Valerie would also try to bargain with June while standing at her bedside.

She offered June anything to wake up. Valerie made many promises that she mentally prepared for June to collect. She promised to buy June things she'd been wanting. She offered to finally make a responsible move to Georgia. Valerie also promised to take care of June, regardless of her condition, needed or not. In spite of the creativity of her promises, nothing worked. She only wavered from June to talk to God.

Valerie's negotiations with God were on-going in the hospital. She offered God her life for June's. There were also countless statements that began "If you will save my sister, I will . . ." or "If June's life is restored I will never . . ."

Valerie had never been one to beg, until now. There she stood pleading for June's life. The obvious rejections of her requests were frustrating. She asked vital questions and received a non answer, which in itself is a response.

A little later in life, Valerie found herself in yet again another dire situation. The circumstance was not as bleak, but desperation filled her heart. In speaking with God, she returned to her prior begging state. This time, she realized through prayer and rosary recitals that her conversation with the Father was being driven by fear. That was never good.

Valerie stopped and revamped her approach because she trusted in the Lord, but wasn't acting like it. Valerie's mind kept revisiting the last time she bargained her life away. The enemy was trying to lead her to a place of uncertainty. She had to focus on her trust and rely on God for the right answer.

Later on she was blessed with acceptance, but before that happened she went through a phase of feeling sorry for June. She was convinced that June regretted missing certain things after she had gone. This became a serious issue as she moved through the grieving process.

Valerie mentally tallied all the events June resented missing and there were many. She would slouch in bed, buried under covers thinking of all the things June would never see.

During this time-frame, there was so much going on that June would have loved. One of the single most important was Barack Obama. She was uncertain if Senator Obama had hit June's radar in 2006, but he had already been in Valerie's sights.

The name Barack Obama stood out to her after he delivered the Keynote Address at the Democratic Convention on July 27, 2004. It was phenomenal. Valerie made sure that she downloaded the speech off the internet. The words he delivered had such an awesome sentiment and she wanted them in her possession. Valerie started listening whenever she heard mention of Obama's name and rushed to read his book, *Dreams from my Father*. She was pleasantly surprised to find the convention speech was located inside of it. *She thought this guy could be president.* June would have loved Obama's charismatic ways and genuine concern for the country.

Once Valerie let go of the hidden anger she possessed regarding June's death, she was able to refine her thinking. She focused on the blessing of their time spent together. Valerie realized that she was not only grieving June, but an old version of herself.

Everyone talks about the person lost and the pain, but no one mentions how death affects the living. There had been no real conversation about how death lingered on within the lives of those left behind. Dying is always spoken about as a transition from life to death to an eternal existence; depending on your belief. What about those who continue to live after an impactful loss? They become different. How are they affecting the world?

Valerie took note of her new self daily. Her transformation began before June died. Inside the hallways of the hospital Valerie was slowly dying too. Sometimes she would miss her prior self, keeping her would have been simpler. She was more complicated and gray. This newer version was stronger, more often black and white and hates to waste time. She could no longer hold important things back nor accept things that she should not. The word "maybe" no longer existed where a definitive could fit.

Valerie lost people in this new space. Sometimes people and things being removed are a blessing, even when it hurts. She learned to acknowledge a range of blessings and move forward, quickly. True loved ones remain. Finding out who really loved her became as simple as limiting access to things and saying no.

Valerie's updated persona was refreshing to many and a disaster to others, but it was still her inside. There were remnants of the old model hanging around, but her whole life needed to change. Positivity was in and negativity was no longer a friend. Valerie embraced her changes and rejoiced looking forward to the unknown. The unfamiliar previously horrified her, but no more.

Not long after June died, Valerie would try and retreat any chance she could, but friends would rally around her and not allow it. They told her when she was staying to herself too much. They chased her as she attempted to run from the world. Valerie's friends spoke to her when she needed to talk, even when it was uncomfortable to do so. Others sat with her in silence when she wouldn't talk. They tolerated continuous one word answers and praised God when those single words turned into phrases. Everyone was astonished when the phrases were finally accompanied by other verbiage and became part of a conversation. Between friends and the ministry group, Valerie found her voice again.

Outside of the occasional setback, Valerie was doing much better. Emotion would come from inside of her and quickly disappear. She learned to take it for what it was worth—a pure expression of love for June. Nearly three years later, to the date, the most solemn feeling circled Valerie's spirit. It was undeniable. She embarked on intensely grim feelings for a few days.

Valerie didn't know why she was so sensitive. She became extremely bothered and couldn't figure out what was happening. She'd been moping around for days unable to deal with anything. She glanced at the calendar and realized it was coming—the day June died.

It was just like Melody said, "As soon as the month of April hits, I become depressed."

Despair swept in and consumed Valerie hopelessly because the date was coming.

In an instance everything was okay, then the whole thing flip-flopped and it was wrong again. This sensation was like a quickening of misery and almost maddening. Thankfully, she was alright, outside of impending sadness on occasion. She had to learn how to deal with it; reaching for God first. Valerie should have gotten professional help. Luckily, she was sustained.

The family was blessed with kind friends. The Petersons were not alone. In fact, many new friends were gained, while others stayed away; intentionally treading lightly.

One of the comments Valerie appreciated the most was when a friend said, "I don't know what to say because I cannot imagine what you're going through, but I'm here for you. Just call if you need anything."

Not another word was spoken, but no other words were necessary. It was clear that Valerie had support and the loss of her sister was important. That acknowledgement honored their friendship.

She has accepted heaven as June's new residence. In that respect, Valerie is happy for June and believes that she is having the time of her life in holy happiness. Sometimes, she doesn't know if she believes it because she needs to or because it is fact. Regardless, coming to that decision, Valerie became more joyful in her own life.

June's death also made Valerie think about her inevitable demise. Previously, like many, she wasn't ready to think about it. Now, that was not an issue. Valerie knew she would have to draft a will, but decided to write a letter first. Valerie thought about what she'd like a letter from June to say and then started. She wrote:

To My Dear Hearts,

I love you, still. Don't worry about a thing because I'm better than I ever knew I could be and you shall be too. Although I'm missing time spent with you in the physical, we remain inside each other's hearts because real love does not die. I sincerely hope that I transitioned from one life to the next peacefully, but if the circumstances were tragic try not to be alarmed. Nobody sleeps eternally without God's permission. I lived the life I was meant.

I have long waited to see those who have passed. I'm reunited with all those who love me. Never forget, your best days are ahead. The ride will be rocky, at times, but glorious. Christ continues to carry all of us, especially through trying times. Allow Him to hold you, always.

You were given everything necessary to survive all things. You will hear bad suggestions both internally and externally, but know that they are only suggestions and you are strong enough to ignore them. Allow God's influence inside of you to shine. You may be in pain, but learn to respect it and recognize that this type of pain comes from love.

Do not embrace it because the pain will consume you if you let it. As swiftly as it appears, it can dissipate. It's okay to shed tears for someone you love your tears are holy and will cleanse you. Strengthen your voice and please seek help if you need it. Cling to the goodness that exists.

As far as arrangements and visiting my grave, do whatever makes things easier for you because I'm forever alright. Don't forget the living. Take care of each other because God is handling me. Don't forget our relationship embrace its new form. Find the beauty that lives in your pain and use it to help others. I want you to be certain of our love for each other and honor it. Become more than you are, now that I may no longer assist you, in person, on your journey.

Commit to your memory that God is good, everyday, including the day I died. Never wonder if I loved you because I did. Know it and stand firm in it. If we argued, we loved each other anyway. That no longer matters so let go of it. True love never dies and we will meet again. Above all, learn to forgive yourself and anyone that has wronged you regardless of what they did; especially when it's hard. Let the Lord take on your burdens.

To my children specifically, if you are well, know that I am too. So walk in God's path and let Jesus usher you towards greatness. A good parent wants to know they have left you in a place of strength. So, from this point on strive to achieve the prominence that God has instilled in you and honor that passion. Here are three p's to live by in life. Remember when you have issues to push through them. Praise His holy name always and pray. I wrote this, I hope it brings you peace.

Jesus

He lives within us
He walks beside us
He speaks living words into our spirit
He breathes for us
He heals us
Pray to His Father
In Jesus' name, Amen

I wish you all happiness while loving you eternally,
Valerie

Strangely, Valerie felt satisfied after signing her letter. She placed it in an envelope and wrote on top of it—for my loved ones. Valerie threw the envelope inside a decorative box filled with an assortment of things. She placed it in her closet on the top shelf and moved back into thoughts of life.

Chapter 16

YEARS after June was killed, the Petersons were told that the trial was going to finally happen. Honestly, they never understood why it was taking so long. They weren't looking forward to being in the courtroom, but it was good to know that things were being handled. They figured the trial would offer much needed closure.

The entire family made plans to be in Georgia for the trial, only to find out it was canceled. Everyone quickly turned in their plane tickets for an airline credit that could be applied to another flight; once another court date was set. The family received another call to justice, only to hear that was canceled too.

Valerie spent time mentally preparing to sit in the courtroom. She attempted to organize her thoughts so that she wouldn't be thrown by what might be said or seen during trial. She knew it was very possible there would be things they'd never seen or heard. After all, some things are not necessary in life, but may need to be said repeatedly for trial purposes.

She worried about the trial's impact on the family. Valerie remembered being in the room with June and Officer Cosby while he took pictures and knew they too would surface. She didn't like that mom and Chuck would have to witness all of that. She also thought about Samantha not having been at the hospital. She didn't witness any of it. Samantha never saw June's face. Valerie liked that one of them had not seen June that way. She also loved that Samantha had a great looking last memory of June's face as it had been throughout her life.

Valerie prayed aloud, "Lord, please help me to be okay during this trial. Please handle this for us."

She had gotten better at speaking to God.

The on-again-off-again court date was planned and canceled a total of six more times. Mom and Samantha made a decision to fly to Atlanta. They went to Georgia to find out what was holding up the process. They promised to alert friends and let family know when to make flight arrangements, instead of depending on the District Attorney.

The District Attorney's office was holding a deposition hearing regarding the case the morning mom and Samantha arrived. They called Theresa and Rick to sit in on it. Mom called New York to explain that a deposition is supposed to determine when the actual trial would occur. God only knows what happened because the next time mom called it was all over. The trial ended swiftly.

Shelly Christopherson was sentenced to 25 years in prison during the hearing and just like that it was over. Most of the family missed the trial. Who knows what 25 years actually meant between time served and the possibility of parole? How much time would she really serve? Regardless, the Petersons hoped that she used the time wisely.

The family members who did not attend the hearing were told very little. The details were important but it became imperative not to further upset mom and Samantha. The questions and answers were quickly aborted. The specifics were not as important as Samantha and the Peterson matriarch are to the family. The protective mode they were in basically translated into not pressing them for information. The family had already been under enough stress.

Valerie had been waiting for the trial for years and now it was over; she missed it. It almost didn't sit right with her, she really wanted to attend; not to pass judgment, but to have justice served and see Ms.

Christopherson again. Valerie wanted to stare in Shelly's face once more and wanted her to see the family again.

Valerie prayed continuously, trying to brace for the unknown. She didn't want to be melodramatic, but it was her intention to attend the trial. Obviously, she wasn't meant to be in the courtroom. Her prayers had been answered. God was good that way—the decision was made.

There was no need for Valerie to worry about how they would be affected. It was done. Time was wasted on something she was never going to attend. Valerie began to actively cast her burdens on the Lord. Time spent worrying can't be regained. Valerie didn't need to be worried about a thing.

Valerie asked God, "What can I do, Father? Please show me the way to heal and make a difference. I will do whatever you say."

This prayer was chanted nonstop, until an answer was received. Valerie didn't like the response, although what needed to be done was clear. It was settled. She would use her plane voucher to visit Shelly Christopherson in prison.

Valerie had never been to a correctional facility. And she didn't really want to be in one now, but she had to speak to Shelly. She was having serious second thoughts while being scanned to move forward for visitation. Having her body searched was like an overdramatic airport scenario gone wrong. Valerie especially found having to lift her bra degrading, but she had come too far to turn back now.

As she sat in the visitation room, at a table waiting, suddenly Valerie became nervous. Beads of sweat formed on her upper lip, a headache was forming and her stomach began to feel queasy. The nauseous feeling grew and Valerie decided this was a bad idea. As she stood up with her hands on the table, pushing her chair back, Shelly was brought into the area. Valerie slowly, sat back down.

Shelly said nothing as she sat down. She simply stared at Valerie. There was no visible recognition in her face. She just sat there wondering why Valerie was there.

Valerie said, "Thank you, for seeing me. I'm Valerie Peterson, June Peterson's sister."

There was no response, only a continuous gawk. This intense unflinching gaze made Valerie want to set it off. Sitting across from Shelly, after what she had done was unsettling. All the raw emotion that was trying to force its way up and out of Valerie's system was making it worse. She stayed calm because she had a message to deliver. Valerie was watching her too.

Valerie said, "Okay. I know this visit is a bit unorthodox, but I have something to say. I'd like to talk to you about finding true beauty within this tragic situation you've caused."

Shelly still didn't say anything, but her face showed intrigue. Her expression changed drastically, letting Valerie know she was listening. Shelly's body language was also telling. She leaned forward in a less intense manner resting her elbows on the table.

Valerie's one person audience had arrived and she acknowledged it by talking further.

Valerie said, "Please do yourself a favor and pay attention. There is good all around you, even here. You just have to find it. I thought about the message my mom sent you in the hospital and prayed about it. In fact, when you think about it, I've learned to pray more intensely and better because of you." Valerie paused, scanned her memories and shook her head then said, "I mean, I've leaned on the Lord like never before because of what you did to my sister. My spiritual center strengthened as you crashed into my life."

Valerie's left eyebrow was raised and her lips were gravitating to the side. She could feel her whole face tensing up and figured she should wrap things up.

"Long story short, Shelly, God has a plan for you. He does for all of us, but you have to be willing to let His glory shine through the rest of your life. Stop letting the devil mask your beauty" Valerie leaned forward and said with some pleasure, "because he's making you look ugly as hell." She continued her ongoing sermon with an attitude, "Are you gonna look for it? Well, that's all I have to say because I'm getting angry up in here. I don't know if you're really hearing me or if you're just gloating over there about being such a bother."

Valerie stood up and turned to leave when a miracle happened.

Shelly asked, "Look for what?"

Valerie turned back around quick. She was surprised to hear Shelly's voice and replied with an attitude, "Excuse me?"

"You asked me if I was gonna look for something. Look for what?

Shelly reverted back to silence and patiently waited for an answer.

Valerie closed her eyes and took a deep breath. When she opened them her hand extended, as if to say wait. She sat down again, holding her head in between her hands and mumbled the "Glory Be" prayer. As the prayer concluded she corrected her posture.

Valerie said, "You're supposed to look for God. He's the beauty that will shine through all the pain you spewed. He's the light in your incarcerated tunnel. He is the antidote to the withdrawal you've hopefully gone through, and the love that will spare your children further neglect." Tears streamed down Valerie's cheeks, but she managed to say, "My sister was sweet perfection. She was like happiness bottled. She brought joy to everyone she met. You're being given a chance through this ill-gotten gift squeezed out of her last breaths to do the same."

Valerie quickly looked around and saw the guards across the room.

She leaned across the table, grabbed Shelly lifting her slightly and yelled, "Make it count! There are lessons to be learned and people for you to save!"

Valerie shoved Shelly back into her seat and couldn't stomach anymore. Valerie turned to leave, but a guard was standing there.

The guard said, "Try that again and you're out of here. You won't be back either."

"That's fine, I'm leaving."

She returned to the prison two more times, each time went better than the last.

Shelly spoke with Valerie, took notes and shared some thoughts. She never fully revealed whether she was on board, but Valerie felt like she was making progress.

During her third and last visit, as she gathered her things to leave, Valerie said, "This is my last visit and I'll leave you with three things. First, it's my sincerest prayer that you choose to make a positive difference going forward. Your life could have been wiped out so easily, but it wasn't. Ask Him why and you'll find your purpose. Second, you need to acknowledge this was no real accident. It was a reality created by the decisions you willingly made. This incident was actually shaped on purpose through your neglect. It could have all been avoided."

Shelly shook her head no.

Valerie continued, "For instance, an accident would be like tripping while holding a glass, but holding it after greasing up your hands and throwing it up into the air to catch is an example of purposeful neglect. You were continuously urging a negative situation to come forth by heavily greasing up on your drugs of choice and then getting into a car. Your wrong choices have deeply affected both our families, as well as countless others. Individual choices matter. And last, if you really do suffer over this, and God forgive me, but I hope that you do. Learn to forgive yourself."

As Valerie left the penitentiary, she hoped to never see Shelly Christopherson again. In her rental car, driving back to the hotel, she couldn't help thinking about choices—hers and everyone else's. She became slightly overwhelmed thinking about how much choices matter.

Back at the hotel, Valerie should have been packing to go home, but she stood in front of a floor length mirror feeling like God had made everyone to interact with everyone else. Strangers continuously touch each other's lives. This philosophy has been shown in movies she loved like *Crash, Babel and Miracle at St. Anna*. She felt like the answer to the universe had just been unlocked and wanted to tell the family.

They didn't even know she had visited Shelly. She thought it was best not to let them know.

The Petersons had all the information they needed. They knew the verdict and the outcome would remain the same—June was gone.

Chapter 17

THE date June passed came again. There was usually a somber mood among everyone that hovered in the air. Usually a bad disposition lingered in the atmosphere for weeks, but especially on that date.

Now it was different somehow. There was a subtle undertone of lighter days. It was unmistakably amazing. No one was really talking about June, but she was present. Extremely bad weather interrupted the family's plan to meet by the side of June's grave.

Valerie didn't want to go with the family, but if mom needed her to stand nearby and pray she should. They would help each other in various ways through those painful moments. Everyone contributed the gift of support through presence; strengthening the family. Previously, mom spoke to Valerie about visiting June.

Valerie quickly said, "That sounds nice mom, but June is in a better place."

Mom stated, "I know that and I know what I believe! I was raised visiting cemeteries with my siblings and your grandmother. We would sit by the gravesite all day sometimes talking to each other or to those we missed. There is still an earthly body in that spot. A body I loved and I pay reverence to it. I will always place flowers where June's body is laid."

"That's beautiful, mom. I can respect that, but for my own sanity, I have to remember as I place flowers that June is in peace elsewhere."

It was vital for each of them to stand strong in their beliefs. There might be times when values cannot be shared, but everyone tried to be in concert. They remembered not to forget each other. Sometimes people become so focused on the ones lost that they fail to remember the living, including themselves. The Petersons tried to keep each other in mind every day. Life is too precious to only share with the nonliving.

No sooner than Valerie had made her peace with the graveside vigil, life threw a curve ball. It's funny how life is sometimes. As soon as you stop resisting, it changes. The weather changed the intended day.

Valerie woke up thankful, but wondered how this day might go with the family. Her morning definitely started right. She woke up just in time to watch her morning television ministries. As usual, she was inspired and left her room with things to incorporate into the day. She hoped that things would continue on this good feeling wave length.

Valerie headed down the stairs for food. Peter and Melody were coming through the front door as she walked down the steps. She was shocked, but instantly happy to see them. It was good seeing Peter today. She walked into the kitchen to find Jan cooking breakfast for everyone.

The family's spirits were high. It was a good day, just as every day should be in one way or another. Valerie went to grab some grub and noticed Theresa coming through the front door. Samantha was already at the table with all our children. The dining room was overcrowded and bustling with love.

Valerie felt blessed having the entire family around, especially all of her living siblings. They were by her side and she thanked God for them. Unfortunately, it's so rare that they're all in the same space, but here they were all together. On a historic family day such as today, they sat among each other a little stronger, better even.

They all still missed June, but she had to be standing among the family today. This breakfast was like no other, something was happening like it had never before during a family gathering. Love was bringing them together.

The family mixed and mingled together wonderfully. When Chuck arrived, he was in a remarkable mood too. Chuck greeted everyone with hugs, kisses and light hearted jokes. He was a hit and everyone loved it. It was clear that everything would indeed be alright.

They'll never get over losing June, but you're not supposed to go through something like that to store it in the back of your mind. It stays up front and center. Either you will use the experience or it will use you. Choose wisely which scenario you would like to experience.

Valerie had encountered so many people that had buried multiple siblings, children and relatives. That is just another reason that she knows she is blessed. Some have gone on to live phenomenal lives helping and spreading love everywhere. While others gave into the anger and hate, ultimately, letting their sorrow destroy them; leaving destruction and pain wherever their journey led.

The Petersons stand strong. They have each other and will continue to for as long as God is willing.

From the desk of Alice Benton
Letter to the Readers

Dear Readers,

Thank you for reading this story. While it is a work of fiction, Beauty in Pain was inspired by a personal tragedy—the loss of my sister, Jennifer. Writing this story has been cathartic. At times, I cried over my laptop, stopping only to pray. It was truly a bitter sweet labor of love.

In her death, Jennifer has become a literal eternal gift that keeps on giving. As such, I will not allow my sister's death to become the very event that stunts my future growth, through depression. I strive for new ways to honor her; I still want to make her proud.

Jennifer has fueled my life and continues to push me to the next level. Jennifer's death urges me to strive for excellence and not waste precious time and energy. It's like the observation deck at the top of the World Trade Center that I will never see. I was convinced that I would go up there eventually. You know, one day. I was wrong. I thought I always had time because I live in New York. Well, time ran out. It was that simple.

If something is important to you cherish it. If someone is significant treasure them, don't wait. Show them all the love and respect they deserve. The time you share, however long is unknown. Jennifer only had 38 years in this world. She was 38 years young.

Our time together was more precious than I ever knew. The missing never stops. Most days, I am well put together and then there are those other ones. I may simply pass "Little House on the Prairie" while channel surfing, a show she loved, and fall apart. All is well though; my tears are a cleansing salute of holiness.

The race is on and only God knows exactly when I will approach my finish line. While I do not know when my end is at hand, I plan to display His glory during all of my laps around the track. Further, it is my job to mark each mile with achievements. It's kind of like that bucket list. Milestones can be marked by quality time shared with loved ones. Actually stop to smell the roses or serve others. Try not to take things for granted. Your loved ones should know how you feel, when you feel it. They shouldn't have to guess about your positive affirmation towards them. I have said many extra I love yous because of this knowledge. I also pay attention when I receive them and they are not always in words.

I have learned that true love conquers all things. It transcends time and death. It is incomparable. True love may change, deepen even, but it never goes away. It survives all things. Love is what makes the world go round, literally. It is what matters. That's why it's alright to mourn. That's why it's okay to take time to grieve, and love is also the main reason to continue to live. It is unconditional and should be embraced where it exists. The person you share it with may not stand before you tomorrow.

Some of the best lessons I have ever learned came from this extremely unfortunate happenstance. I have heard people say throughout my life, what doesn't kill you will make you stronger. I've added, don't let anything take you, except God. If a circumstance arises where there appears to be a choice to live or die, rise and fight on toward life.

Show God that even when a situation seems bleak and there seems no way out, you are worthy of the life He has given. Demonstrate that you know you are not alone and willingly accept any help He sends you. I suspect that when it is truly your time, no choice exists. When my race is up I will be ready, but not a second before because God is always on time.

Ask yourself, what are the things that I want people to know? What should I try in my lifetime? What is my mission? Once you find the life changing answers to these questions, start your own wonderful race. Also, be prepared for two things. First, we never have all the answers. Sometimes we need help in our discovery. We were not meant to go through this life alone. Second, a vast majority of breakthroughs can be found inside our pain. Examine the struggle that drives you. Thankfully, I have found in my pain, the grace of God and peace beyond what I could have achieved on my own.

My mission is to help others realize that God resides inside us in all situations. He doesn't pick and choose. He remains our Father always. These things that feel so tragically like the end of the world, may very well be the end of the world as we know it, but not necessarily the finale. It can be the beginning of a new and magnificent world. Sometimes a better one if we give it a chance to thrive. This new world will possess revolutionary potential to charter a better existence.

After, such a personal earthquake, I much later became aware of some things that I didn't fully realize I wanted to do; until it was time. My first book, *Black Love: A Book of Poetry & Love* was one of those things. I have even become aware of things I have been doing my whole life that were made to assist my current ventures. That realization has strengthened my appreciation for all that I do and forged an overall excitement for my future. Do you see? God is good even when we don't recognize His presence.

Last, but not least, I have learned that life itself is good, regardless of the events one has to endure. Waking up is a gift to be treasured. Thank you, Jesus. Living to see another day is no small feat and should be valued. Making it to another day is a chance to improve upon your life. A higher-quality of life is waiting around the bend. Remember your perception is everything. Never forget God's goodness and continually through it all, praise His holy name.

May God bless and keep you always!

About the Author

ALICE Benton is a poet and author. As a writer, she doesn't necessarily stick to any particular literary genre. She possesses a B.A. from the College of New Rochelle and a M.S. Ed. from Fordham University.

Beauty in Pain is Ms. Benton's first novel. Her second novel, *Autumn's Five Seasons* which was inspired by her first book, *Black Love: A Book of Poetry & Love*, is scheduled to come out at the end of 2011. She also looks forward to the production of her play, *What God Gives Me*, and is working continuously on many other projects. For information on upcoming events and what's next, please visit her website at www.alicebenton.com. Ms. Benton also has a blog called Alice Benton's Blog, the web address is www.alicebentonsblog.blogspot.com.

Would you like to have the author speak at an event? Please email your request and type speaking engagement in the Subject.

Alice Benton
P.O. Box 80130
Brooklyn, NY 11208

Email: avbenton@gmail.com